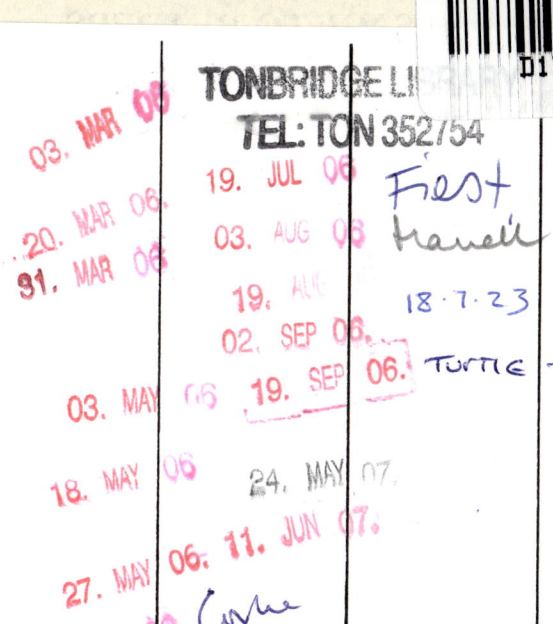

DANGEROUS JOURNEY

To Alice Foster, Jim Peterson's proposal of marriage from Australia is a passport to a better life. Full of hope, she arrives in Fremantle with her young brother, Tom, to be met by notorious gambler Frank Crossley, who is looking for cheap labour. Alice's dream turns to nightmare — until she falls in love with handsome surgeon Ned McCartney. With Ned's help, she escapes the bondage of the Crossley ranch and learns the secret of Jim Peterson's disappearance.

JOYCE JOHNSON

DANGEROUS JOURNEY

Complete and Unabridged

LINFORD
Leicester

First published in Great Britain in 1995

First Linford Edition
published 2005

British Library CIP Data

Johnson, Joyce, *1931* –
    Dangerous journey.—Large print ed.—
    Linford romance library
    1. British—Australia—Fiction
    2. Australia—Emigration and immigration—
    Fiction 3. Love stories 4. Large type books
    I. Title
    823.9′14 [F]

    ISBN 1–84395–700–0

Published by
F. A. Thorpe (Publishing)
Anstey, Leicestershire

Set by Words & Graphics Ltd.
Anstey, Leicestershire
Printed and bound in Great Britain by
T. J. International Ltd., Padstow, Cornwall

This book is printed on acid-free paper

1

Alice Foster bit her lip and concentrated on the linen sleeves her overseer, Martha Green, had ripped from the nearly completed shirt. It was the fourth time in a week her sewing had been criticised — by Miss Green every time.

The older woman's eyes glittered with spite as she glared at Alice's bent head.

'Shoddy work again, miss. Stay behind and set those sleeves properly. I'll inspect the tackings before you stitch them proper. These garments are sold abroad, and Rivington's have high standards. If you can't do better, you'll have to go. I can't imagine how you got a job here in the first place. Plenty of young women queueing up for work, don't you forget that.'

Martha Green walked away down the

narrow aisle between the work tables in the poorly-lit room, her ramrod back exuding satisfaction at Alice's discomfiture.

Quietly, Alice picked up the sleeves. For some reason Martha Green resented her, and wanted to be rid of her. It wasn't the quality of her work, for she knew she was a first-class seamstress, but if Miss Green had decided Alice wasn't suitable, it was only a matter of time before she got the sack.

In the last decade of the nineteenth century there was an unending supply of cheap labour — men and women desperate for work, particularly in the sweatshops of London's East End. Alice Foster was particularly desperate, even for the low wage of ten pence for a twelve-hour day, or longer if Mr Rivington had orders to meet.

She quickly finished the work on hand for the day, then deftly retacked the sleeves which had been near perfection in the first place. Daylight had long since been defeated in its attempt to shed a more cheerful light in the gloomy work-shed. Economy kept the gas light at the lowest possible level, and Alice's eyes were prickling with exhaustion well before she'd finished.

Martha Green was unable to find fault on the second attempt — maybe even she wanted to be rid of the dreary work day. There'd be plenty of future opportunities to catch out Miss Pretty Alice! With a surly nod, she released the young girl, but it was an hour past the usual finishing time before Alice and her friend and workmate, Lizzie, left the premises.

Bonnetted and shawled against the freezing night fog, the girls left the dingy alleyway where Rivington's girls stitched the immaculate shirts and garments which had made him a fortune. They shivered in the cold, their breath making vapour clouds which thickened the dense murk even more, but Alice's troubles were greater than the pain of her numb fingers and sore eyes.

'It'll not be long before she sacks me. I can feel it in my bones. Then what'll we do?'

'Your bones?' Lizzie laughed. It was a childhood joke between them, Alice's reliance on her bones to predict events. 'Not the most reliable things to go on. Your dad's no better?'

Alice shook her head. 'Worse — since his last illness. He can't find any work. Bertha's tried to, but someone has to look after the boys. They all need shoes, and I don't want Tom to leave school. But if I lose my job, he'll have to. Why does Miss Green hate me so? I've never done anything to harm her.'

Lizzie gave her friend a sidelong glance — it was easy to see what Alice had done! 'You're young and pretty, that's what and everyone likes you — which can't be said of old Martha.'

'But you're pretty, too — and the other girls. Why me?'

Lizzie shrugged. It was hard for her to define Alice's quality. They'd been friends all their lives — she just knew that when Alice was around, life seemed much more cheerful. She had a warmth and spontaneity which somehow cast a lustre on their drab lives. It was unusual to see her so downcast. If Alice Foster wasn't her usual cheerful self, what hope for the rest of them!

Alice's mother had died six years earlier, and since then the family fortunes had taken a rapid down-turn. Alice and her younger sister, Bertha, had looked after their three small brothers, but when Dick Foster had become ill and could no longer support his family, Alice had to become the sole breadwinner, leaving Bertha to cope with the household chores.

Lizzie cast around for something cheerful to say to her friend.

'I've heard there's a big order come in. Mr Rivington'll need all the workers he can get. Old Martha'd never dare get rid of you. And Bertha does out-work for him, too, so that'll be some-thing . . . '

'Bertha's got so much to do, and since Dad's been home, he's difficult — he just hates not having work. Bertha should be working, too, and going to night classes — that's the only way we'll get better work . . . ' Alice paused, and a desperate note put a bitter edge in her voice. 'Lizzie, sometimes I think we'll never get out of this trap. It takes all our efforts just to survive. There must be more to life. What sort of future is there for any of us?'

'Don't fret, please. Something'll turn up. I feel it — in my bones!' She squeezed Alice's arm, trying to sound more cheerful than she felt.

Alice was contrite. 'I'm sorry. Don't mind me. I shouldn't be worrying you. It's all Martha Green's fault. We must forget her. D'you know, I do think something nice is about to happen. Maybe a hot supper. Isn't that a cheerful idea?'

The girls had reached the street

where they'd lived a few doors away from each other all their lives, and where they knew all their neighbours, too. The familiarity of community, however poverty-stricken, warmed them both.

Alice felt a surge of better spirits as they neared home. 'Something good,' she repeated, 'I can feel it in my bones!'

They both laughed, and went indoors to their respective houses.

'Hello — I'm home,' Alice called out, her nose telling her that something good was up. A savoury smell hit her nostrils, and at the same time, her young brother, Tom, hurtled to meet her.

'Alice — you're so late. Something's up, but Dad wouldn't tell until you came home. He sent me out for pies and ale and . . . ' His words tumbled out, too fast for sentences. 'He's been excited. Won't say — and there's a letter — from Australia. Who do we know there?' He slowed, voice awe-struck, eyes round. 'Australia, Alice. Who could that be from? Pies, too!'

'So you said. It must be an occasion.' Alice took off her overshoes, unwound her shawl, unpinned her bonnet, and faced her father, who'd come out to meet her, with a smile, glad to see him so lively and clear-eyed. 'There. Now I'm ready.'

She followed him into the kitchen, where a scrubbed table was set with plates and cutlery. Bertha, four years younger than Alice, was busy at the stove; the three boys, Tom, Billy and young Harry, were already seated. They were eleven, eight and six, and tried to help the family purse by running errands, earning pennies here and there.

Dick Foster knew his family lived on a knife edge. Their existence was poverty stricken, but they just managed to survive. He knew real deprivation and separation was only a hair's breadth away and, accordingly, his life was lived in constant fear. Not tonight though — tonight there was hope — in the letters. He felt he was head of the

8

household, and once more, in charge of the Fosters' future.

'Bertha, look sharp, now,' he commanded. 'Your sister's home. You can serve the tea now.'

Bertha, a small, fragile-looking girl, sliced pie on to plates, cutting hunks of bread to go with it. She spoke to Alice.

'Dad's been impossible since the packet came. Wouldn't tell us a thing until you came home. It must be from Jim Peterson. He's the only person we know who's ever been out of London, let alone England!'

'Hush up and eat your tea. Enjoy the treat. It isn't often we have one, so make the most of it.'

Dick picked up his knife and refused to say another word until every last morsel of food had been cleaned from all the plates. He watched Bertha and Alice tidy the table, took a deep swallow of ale and finally produced a brown envelope.

'Just imagine,' he pointed to the foreign stamps, 'all that way. It must be more than ten thousand miles across the seas. A letter from Australia!'

'Dad!' Alice exploded. 'Are you going to tell us what this is all about? If not, I'd just as soon not know. The tea was lovely, but Bertha and I have lots to do before bedtime. So, if you're going to keep up the mystery, we'll be getting on.' She got up, affecting nonchalance.

Dick knew his moment of glory was over — he understood his daughter. Alice could be as doggedly determined as her father. 'The letter's from Jim, Jim Peterson, your sweetheart, Alice. He's written to you, too.'

'He's not my sweetheart. How could he possibly be, when I haven't clapped eyes on him for five years — and never a word in between?'

'He used to be. You mooned after him long enough, and when he went away you never stopped crying. Pined to death nearly!'

'I was only just turned fifteen.'

Alice spoke with unaccustomed sharpness, as the five years rolled back.

It was partly true; as a young girl, she'd been bowled over by Jim Peterson, a good-looking young man, four years older than she was. He always seemed to have plenty of money, and constantly bought her small presents. She remembered, too, with a half smile, that he was always laughing. She could see his brown eyes now, crinkling at the corners, teasing her, joking that he was going to marry her when she'd caught up in years. She'd loved the thought. Being married to Jim had appeared a wonderful prospect when she was fifteen.

But, as Alice started to blossom into an attractive woman, her mother became ill, and all her concern was to help her endure a long and painful illness. Jim hadn't been around much when Mabel Foster took sick, until one evening when he came round and told them he was embarking for Australia the next morning. Alice blanched at the memory, could still hear her childish wail.

'But you can't — not now Mother's ill. I'll . . . ' She'd trailed off, shocked that he'd never mentioned his plans to her. She couldn't say, 'I'll be needing you.'

'I know. It's sudden, but I've no option. I'll explain one day. You're so young. Alice, don't cry. I'll — I'll write. Promise.'

Something troubled him — there was no laughter in his eyes that day. His visit lasted a bare five minutes, and he couldn't wait to leave. There'd been no word from him since.

Alice blinked away the painful memory, long since tucked away. 'So, what does he say — five years later? Can I see my letter?'

Her father looked uncomfortable. 'He wrote, asking me to speak first — and the rest of the family — it concerns them, too. This could be our chance — a new start for all of us.'

'Dad, what are you talking about? What's he written that's made you so wild?' Alice hadn't seen him so animated since her mother had died. Something, someone, had fed hope into his life. She prayed it wasn't false hope.

He made an effort to speak more calmly.

'In Australia, Jim's done well. Better than he ever could do here. There's so much out there. Look . . . ' He pointed to the window, at the black square of night, where the fog pressed and crouched like a waiting predator. 'I can't survive many more winters in this climate. Where Jim is, there's sunshine. Always, he says. Look.' He took sheets of paper and documents from the envelope with the strange-looking stamps. 'Read. Read what he says. He's made all the arrangements. You can see what he's written to you, but look here first.'

'What? Dad, what nonsense is this? What's Australia to do with our family? We can't go there.'

'But we can. Or at least you can. Jim's sent you a ticket for a steamship, passenger class. And extra money, too, to get some things for the journey. Ninety days it'll take, and when you get there it'll be hot, Jim says.'

'Ticket? Journey? Are you mad? Bertha, do you know what it means?'

Her sister looked from one to the other. The boys sat quiet as mice for once, aware that something momentous was in the air. 'The money draft — it's in your name. I suppose Jim wants you to go to Australia.'

'But why? What for?' Alice burst out in astonishment.

Dick said quickly, 'As his wife, of course. He wants you to be married — in Australia. Isn't that good?' He saw his daughter's face, and stopped.

'His wife! In Australia? He wants me to live there — with him?'

Dick's excitement died a little, but he nodded and pushed the letters towards her. There was silence in the small room. A coal dropped in the hearth.

Tom's voice rang out firmly. 'You can't.'

'You live here — with us.' Billy and Harry spoke in unison.

Alice looked at her sister, but Bertha avoided her eyes.

'There's nothing here,' Dick repeated fiercely, 'nothing! He says we're to go out as well later. All of us. We can get government-assisted passages — as soon as you're settled, and there's a place. Jim's struck gold — at somewhere called Kalgoorlie. He's made all the arrangements. I'm to telegraph the P & O office in Fremantle when a passage has been arranged. He'll meet you, but if he can't for some reason — there's even an address. Look.' His thumb ran down the letter. 'Care of Crossley Ranch, Near Northam. The train goes near there. Jim's covered everything. He must want you to go very much.'

Every time he looked at the papers, Dick's excitement rekindled. It was what he'd always dreamed of — a good life for his family — a chance! 'If it wasn't for this blooming chest of mine

I'd have been there, too. We'd be set up by now.'

Alice's spirits sank. It was all wild dreams. She looked at him with pity.

'Of course I can't go. It's out of the question. Dad, you must see that.'

'Why not?'

'I can't. I don't love Jim Peterson. And I can't leave you all here.'

Despair made Dick cruel. He lifted his head and looked coldly at her.

'It'd be one less mouth to feed if you went.'

Alice's hand flew to her throat. It was as though he'd hit her.

'Dad!' Bertha's sharp command rang out.

In the heavy silence, Dick stood up. 'I can't say more. I forget — you're the breadwinner. Maybe it's me should go — out of your way!' Disappointment aged his face, killed the glow. He'd been so sure that Alice would jump at the chance. She was just a slave of Rivington's here in London, and always would be. 'That's that then. You won't

16

even read his letter?'

'Of course I will, Dad. Give me a chance. It was just — well, such a shock. A surprise, after all this time. I haven't thought of Jim for years. I can't marry someone I don't love, can I?'

'What's love to do with it?' he replied bitterly. 'Don't forget, beggars can't be choosers — but even beggars can take a chance if it's offered on a plate. I'm going out now. Talk to your sister about it. And for goodness' sake, girl, read the letters.' Defiantly, he walked out, and minutes later they heard his rasping cough fighting for breath in his fog-filled lungs.

The sisters cleared away, and saw a subdued trio of boys into bed. Tom looked anxious. His good-night hug was fierce. He whispered to Alice, 'You wouldn't go — without telling me?'

'What an idea. And I shan't go without your say so,' she joked, trying to cheer them both.

She went downstairs, her brain whirling. Bertha had made some tea while Alice read the letter Jim had written to her father. She re-read it, then passed it to her sister.

'See what you think, Bertha. He makes it sound fine. Seems he struck gold. There was a big find at Kalgoorlie. He wants to settle with a family and friends. Hopes Dad and Mother will persuade me — Bertha, he doesn't even know Mother's dead!'

'How could he? Jim was an orphan. One of his reasons for going, surely? He'd no relatives here to keep him up with news.'

As Bertha took the letter, Alice recalled her sister's childish adoration of Jim Peterson, who'd always been ready to play a game with her in the old days. She could visualise him now, tossing the small child in the air, hear the squeals of delight, see the small hands clutching his hair.

'You don't think I should go?' Alice asked incredulously when Bertha finally raised her head. 'To an unknown country. Marry someone I hardly know? Leave the family?'

'Lots of girls do. I read about some Irish girls. They answered an advertisement for wives for men who'd emigrated. Their lives were so poor in Ireland.'

'But that's dreadful. They'd just be unpaid housekeepers,' Alice replied.

'At least they'd eat.'

'We're not starving. Maybe you should go!' Alice was hurt by Bertha's acquiescent mood, as though she, too, wanted to be rid of that extra mouth.

'He asked you — not me. Perhaps you should read what he says to you.'

'All right. I will,' Alice said, unfolding the letter.

The sisters sat, one on each side of the hearth. Bertha's head was bent to her mending but, from time to time, she glanced across at Alice, her expression unfathomable.

The letter was dated five months earlier — post-stamped Fremantle, Western Australia. Jim's writing was

19

harder to decipher in this letter, as though the letter to her father had taxed all his writing powers, but gradually she became accustomed to it, and more and more absorbed.

Dearest Alice,

You will have a shock — to hear from me after all these years, and I cannot explain my long silence in this letter. I hope to do so when I see you, which I sincerely hope will be within this twelve-month coming. I have thought often of you and I hope you have thought of me, too. You were so upset when I left, I take this as a sign of your affection for me which, I trust, has not changed with the years. I took you for a constant girl, not a trifler.

I could not send for you before. The early years were hard, and I often despaired, but with the gold hit, things have changed. You will see from the money and ticket that I mean you to travel in style as cabin passenger, not as an ordinary emigrant. Your family can join us later if they wish. It would be good to have friends and family here. It has been lonely, but not now, with the prospect of you coming out. I know this is taking a chance — you may even be walking out, or married. If so, have the money as a wedding present from me. But, in my bones, as you used to say, I feel you're still free for me.

Alice, we can have a good life here in this new country. You always were a worker and that's what we need. I have explained matters to your father. Never fear, we will be married just as soon as you set foot off the boat. I hope to have a prosperous farm spread for you and me to work together. What a joy. It will be very different from London's East End — but we would have no chance there. I hope to see you in Fremantle, and look forward to calling you Mrs Alice Peterson. Make me so happy by agreeing to this proposal.

Yours affectionately, Jim Peterson.

Alice dropped the letter on her lap. A sense of Jim's presence came strongly from it, but it was a strange letter — almost business-like; affectionate — yes, but of love — not a word. But what else could she possibly have expected? It was so long ago, and Jim had never been one for showing his deeper thoughts. Always laughing, joking, how well did she really know him?

Bertha asked, 'Well? What are you going to do?'

Alice thought a while before she answered. 'I don't know. I honestly don't know what to do now.'

Bertha got up and raked the embers in the grate. 'Time we went up. There's no more coal. We couldn't afford it — not as well as pies.'

Her blank, hopeless expression made Alice despair. Her father was right. There was no future for them here. Was it selfish to turn down an opportunity of escape? She lit a stub of candle from the dying ashes, and put her arm around her sister's shoulders.

'Cheer up, Bertha. There's a lot of fight left in the Foster family. I'll sleep on Jim's — er — proposition.' Try as she might, she couldn't think of it as a proposal!

2

The next morning, nothing was said about Jim Peterson, or Australia. The freezing cold numbed tongues as well as spirits. Bertha had managed to scrape together some kindling and dusty coal, but the heat barely touched them as they huddled together with the boys to breakfast on luke-warm tea and bread.

Dick Foster stayed upstairs. Bertha told Alice he had an appointment later in the day to see about a night watchman's job.

Alice was horrified. 'But he can't be out in the night air in this weather.'

'I shouldn't worry. There'll be hundreds of others turning up as well, fitter and younger than Dad, but it gives him an hour or two of hope, and somewhere to go during the day. Alice, don't forget to ask about work for me at Rivington's.'

'Lizzie says there's a big order in, so maybe we'll be lucky.' Alice spoke more cheerfully than she felt. If Martha Green had anything to do with it, she'd probably keep Bertha off the list of outworkers altogether.

Morning had still to lighten the dark when she went into the cold, Tom walking along with her the short distance to Lizzie's house. She looked fondly at the young boy.

'Mind your teacher today now,' she said. 'I want good reports from school.'

Tom scuffed his shoes on the cobbles. 'I've got errands to do for Mrs Potts first. That'll make me late, and then I'll be in trouble. I might not go to school at all.' He peered up at Alice, an unusual defiance in his expression.

She stopped, put her hands on his shoulders, and said severely, 'You'll go to school, Tom Foster. If Mrs Potts' errands aren't done before the school bell, then you'll have to do them after school. It's important not to miss lessons. You'll never get decent work without proper schooling.'

His pale face glimmered up at her in the dawning, grey daylight, his eyes troubled. 'You won't be here to see. You'll be in Australia.'

'Tommy, I'm not going today, and it was just an idea. Of Jim Peterson's and Dad — '

The young boy interrupted. 'You all seem pretty sure it's settled.'

'Not at all. I haven't had my say yet. Now, here we are at Lizzie's, so run back now, and Tom, promise me you will go to school today.'

'I will — if you promise to take me to Australia with you.'

Tom's expression was so fierce, Alice couldn't help laughing. 'And what would you do there?' she teased.

'Look after you — and help to make our fortune, so that Dad and the rest could join us. Promise, Alice. Cross your heart.'

Alice's smile died. He was in deadly

earnest. She bent and kissed his cheek.

'I can't promise anything, because I don't know, but I will think about it if I do decide to go. Will that do?'

He nodded reluctantly.

'And you'll be in school today?' she pressed.

Tom turned back towards the house.

'I'll think about it,' he called, over his shoulder.

Alice sighed. How could she possibly even contemplate leaving young Tom?

It was hard to concentrate on her stitching, but Martha Green's eagle eye watched her every movement, and it wasn't until the brief dinner break that Alice was able to tell Lizzie about the letters from Australia.

'Australia! Jim Peterson! Well, well. You were very fond of him years ago. Aren't you pleased? Lucky you, to get out of this rat-hole.'

Alice was shocked by her friend's assumption.

'You think I should go, too? Dad wants me to, and I think Bertha does.

Seems everyone's desperate to be rid of me.'

'Don't look so upset. You know that's not true, but it's such a chance. That's why your dad's so keen. Mine'd be doing my packing this morning if someone sent for me. He's always on about emigrating. Mum won't though, so there's no chance for me either.'

'Bertha says that men out there are advertising for wives.'

'Really!' Lizzie's eyes were saucer-round over her mug of tea. 'Tell me more.'

'You wouldn't! Not now you're walking out with Peter Bruce.'

'I would. You just watch me. If it wasn't for Pete — '

'But — to go and marry a total stranger — '

'It's all a lottery anyway. Who's to say Pete and I'll get on together in life? Not much hope, I'd say, around here.'

Lizzie was number six of ten children; three had left home, and she was expected to marry and move out if her man had work, leaving more room for the remaining half dozen. She had a grittily realistic view of her own future.

'Perhaps I can even persuade Pete to think about emigrating. That'd be fun, all out there together. And, if Jim's done so well, he could maybe give us a helping hand. All one happy family out in the sunshine! Alice Foster, you're a lucky girl, and you can tell that dried-up old Martha Green what she can do with her job. But just for now we'd best get back to the bench — just in case you're mad enough to decide to stay on here.'

Through the rest of the working day Alice's brain raced round in circles. Was Jim's offer the answer? Everyone else seemed to think so. Life in the East End of London appeared to be so desperate, anywhere else must be better. She remembered the story of the Irish girls. But Alice was an optimist, and in spite of the family's troubles, believed that everything would eventually turn out for the best. Maybe she was wrong.

Things didn't just happen — it was up to her to make them happen — seize the chance, and join Jim Peterson on the other side of the world. After all, there was nothing to lose — she could always come back. But even Alice had to concede that, once cast, it would be hard to reverse the throw of the dice. Did she have the courage to make that throw?

'Alice Foster, dream in your own time, not Rivington's. We don't pay you to stare out of the window.'

Alice jumped, flushed, and bent to her needle. Would there be Martha Greens in Australia? No — there she'd be a married woman, and no-one would have the right to treat her like a schoolgirl. Jim, she was sure, would be an easy-going husband. He'd always been such fun.

Her spirits began to rise. Lizzie was right — she was lucky to have the chance of a different life. She concentrated on thinking positively, and determined that on Saturday, her half-day off, she'd go to the library and look up all the books on Australia. Tom could help her — and then the most startling idea of all came to her. Of course, Tom could go with her. It would be his chance, too. If Jim was doing so well, there'd be no problem, and Tom could go to school all day and every day. Hadn't Jim said the entire family would eventually join them? Tom would be a little early, that was all. The first thing she'd look up about Australia would be how their school system worked!

As Martha Green began another approach run to Alice's work table she was put off her stride when her victim said with a broad smile, 'Would you like to check these shirts, Miss Green. I think I'm nearly through here.'

★ ★ ★

When Alice arrived home later that evening there was a glowing fire in the grate and the smell of frying meat in the air. Before she could announce her decision, Bertha told her that their father, surprisingly, had got the job as nightwatchman, and was to start that very night.

'He's upstairs getting ready. We've borrowed some of Jim's money, against Dad's wage, for coals and dinner. Don't discourage him, Alice, he's so pleased with himself — ' She stopped as a fit of coughing racked the house. 'He'll be all right,' she continued swiftly. 'It's partly an indoor job, and it's better for him than doing nothing — even if it doesn't last that long.'

The coughing was stifled and stopped, and five minutes later Dick came downstairs, dressed in his only good suit of clothing. He had a jaunty air, and rubbed his hands and sniffed.

'Smells good, Bertha. Alice, you've heard the news. I've got some work. I'm off — after tea.'

'You shouldn't be out at night at all — but never mind. It won't be for long. I've decided, Dad. I will go to Australia

— and — ' It was difficult to say, it sounded so strange. 'I will marry Jim Peterson, and we'll all be together out there as soon as possible. Then you'll be able to help Jim with the land in the fresh air and sunshine.' She saw Tom's face and said quickly, 'And, if I can arrange it, I'd like Tom to come with me — as an advance party!'

Alice's decision had been made impulsively, on an instinct that the future could be no more poverty stricken than the life they were living, and on the fear she felt for her father's health. It was to be an act of rescue for the whole family, and as the days of preparation went by, she became more and more convinced it was a family move.

If she had looked more closely at Jim's letters she might have realised that his intention was geared to herself alone — not to the entire Foster clan. Though he had mentioned the possibility of them eventually emigrating, it was more to persuade Alice than a desire to be surrounded by her relatives.

She fought down any doubts and threw herself wholeheartedly into the project. She conceived a grand plan. Boldly, she by-passed Martha Green, marched into Mr Rivington's office, proffered her resignation, and asked that Bertha might be taken on in her place. The old man, charmed by her lively prettiness and engaging manner, agreed on the spot.

The two sisters swapped rôles, and Alice became free during the day to make her preparations for leaving England. She negotiated with the steamship company to cash in her open, second-class passage cabin ticket of two lower deck berths, and wrote to Jim, care of the P & O office in Fremantle, Western Australia, that she would be leaving London on the first of May and her expected arrival date was August the tenth, sailing on the steamship Pathan. Her young brother, Tom, would be travelling with her.

She looked at the bald, business-like

details of her letter, conjured up a mental image of Jim, remembered she was going to Australia to marry him, and added, with some misgivings:

I was glad to have your letter and be assured of your affection and remembrance of me. I am pleased to join you in Australia, and hope we shall all have a fine life in the new country. Father, and the rest, are looking forward to it also. Yours affectionately. Alice Foster.

She hesitated over the last sentence, but was too transparently honest not to put Jim clearly in the picture. He may well be getting more than he'd bargained for, but there would be time for him to telegraph any protest about Tom's inclusion should he have any. To make doubly sure, she wrote a note to him, care of the Crossley Ranch, simply giving the date of her arrival in Fremantle, and the name of the ship.

In her few spare hours she went to the lending library and read everything she could about Australia, and gradually a broad picture of the land of opportunities grew in her mind. She read of hardships encountered by the pioneers, the difficulties of climate and terrain, but she was more exhilarated than daunted. It would be a challenge, and Jim had said it was fine.

She spent the last few weeks at home in a mood of cheerful anticipation, trying to curb Tom's growing excitement as well as tending to the two smaller boys. Her father was doggedly sticking to his nightwatchman's job, but Alice saw it as a grim struggle, and she prayed he would get through the rest of the winter without severe illness. Bertha seemed happy enough at Rivington's and experienced no trouble with Martha Green. It seemed, to Alice, that the family had already said goodbye to her in their minds, and would hardly miss her, but, on the appointed day of sailing, she saw the depth of their emotion, and knew it was for her sake, and Tom's, they had maintained a nonchalant attitude, a pose they were unable to keep up when it came to the moment of parting.

Ironically, the first day of May was a brilliantly warm, spring day, and Alice's street of small, terraced houses looked cosy and familiar. Lizzie's family, and most of the neighbours, turned out to wave and cheer as the Fosters piled into an open cart Dick had hired to take baggage and family to the docks. The tin trunk with all the new clothes Alice had made was strapped to the back.

She and Tom had a valise each which they clutched on their knees. To Alice, the departure was unreal, as though it was happening to someone else. A part of her stood on the doorstep of her home watching her other self saying goodbye to the people she had known all her life.

There were tears in Lizzie's eyes as she hugged her friend.

'Mind you write — straightway, and tell me all about it. I've already put the idea into Pete's head, and he didn't say no. Best of luck.'

Dick flicked the reins and the horse

set off at a smart pace over the cobbles. Alice took a last look back at the street. There was no turning back now, but would she ever see it again?

Soon they were by the P & O pier, waiting for the steam launch which would take Alice and Tom out to the SS Pathan, which they could clearly see lying mid-river between Gravesend and Tilbury. Dick, back on the London docks, was in his element. He loved the hustle and bustle of departing and arriving ships, whether passenger or cargo, and gave them a running commentary on all the activity. Alice was silent; Tom held her hand tightly.

'See, over there,' Dick was saying, 'there's the tug from Blackwell. These are mainly emigrants.'

'What are we then?' his eldest son asked.

'Well, Tom, you and Alice are emigrants, too, but you're paying your own fares — at least Jim Peterson is. These people in the tug are being paid for by the government.' He turned to

Alice reassuringly. 'Jim'll be in Fremantle to meet you.'

'I hope so, Dad. It's strange that we haven't heard from him again.'

'I expect there's letters on the ship now that have missed you. The mail takes a long time from outlying districts. You mustn't worry, girl.'

'I'm not.' Alice's reply was truthful. The voyage was to be an adventure, and she was determined to make the most of it. Once on the ship . . . it was just the parting that was so hard to bear. She looked away from the dear faces of her brothers and sister and watched a group of passengers about to board the steam launch. Their turn next.

Her breath left her body as she saw a tall figure, back towards her, embracing a young girl, who was unashamedly weeping.

'Jim!' Alice gasped out.

The man turned towards her, and of course, it wasn't Jim. The broad shoulders and dark, curling hair were similar, and there was something about the set of the head, but this man's eyes were a deep, dark-blue, whereas Jim's were brown. Jim was an East Ender; this man was of a different quality, taller, too, she noted, as he disengaged himself from the young woman clinging so tightly to him. He looked directly at Alice, a puzzled frown on his face.

Embarrassed, she flushed, averted her eyes and shook her head slightly. Still keeping his gaze on her, the tall figure took off his hat and inclined his head towards her, a faint smile curving his lips. Then the young woman touched his arm and reclaimed his attention.

Alice wondered who was leaving and who was saying goodbye to whom. Then the man embraced another, older woman, shook hands with several men, and stepped into the waiting launch. A few yards out, the stranger unfastened his cloak and waved to the group left behind. Head tilted upwards, his sweeping gaze encompassed Alice and her family, and she wondered how she could possibly have imagined the man to be at all like Jim.

They watched the launch to the ship, saw the passengers disembark and climb aboard the big steamer, and all too soon it was back at the pier, ready for the next load.

The people who'd waved goodbye to the stranger were still on the quay, the girl wiping her eyes now. The older woman put her arm around her, and Alice heard her say, 'Now, Tilly, you couldn't go with him this time. Maybe later — '

The reply was muffled in the comforter's shoulder, as they made their way back to the pier, passing close to Alice.

Then there was no time for speculation as to what the relationship was between Tilly and the man already aboard the steamship. Alice forgot about them as she hugged her family, each one in turn.

Dick held her tightly. 'I'm sorry to see you go, but it's for the best. And we'll follow — I'm sure of it. Look out for Tom — and you, my lad.' His other arm encircled the boy. 'Look after your sister. You're the man of the family now, and I look to you to take care of things. Jim'll treat you right. He always had a soft spot for you. I wouldn't be letting you go if I didn't think that.'

There was no more time. Down the pier steps, a seaman's proffered hand, into the launch, and already the sunlit stretch of Thames was widening and separating Alice and Tom from the rest of the Foster family. They waved and waved, until finally the launch reached the mother ship, and Tom and Alice were helped aboard. Eagerly they turned for a last look. One final wave, shouts of goodbye drifted in the clear air, and Dick Foster turned his depleted family around and slowly walked back up the dock.

A lead weight settled on Alice's stomach, but for Tom's sake she smiled brightly and clasped him to her side.

'Here's the start of the adventure,

Tommy. Won't it be fun on the ship? Let's see where we're going to live for these next months.'

Alice's heaviness persisted until all the passengers and cargo had been loaded on to the ship, but as the engines began to vibrate and the funnels belched out smoke, excitement took over, and when the boat finally began to move with a hooting and whistling, she felt positively light-hearted.

It was all such a novelty — there was so much to take in. A steward showed them to their quarters, down-graded to pay the cost of both of them, but comfortable enough. Alice had read of the terrible conditions endured in the crowded and insanitary quarters of the early sailing ships by the pioneers and settlers, many of whom had died before ever reaching the shores of the new continent. But the later ships, built for steam, were better equipped to carry immigrants. Indeed, had Alice travelled without Tom, and kept her second-class cabin ticket, her voyage would have been a positive luxury trip compared to her home life.

As it was, she and Tom travelled as lower-deck passengers but, even here, they found very tolerable arrangements. The deck was divided into large rooms, with air portholes and lockers for each berth. There were twenty berths in Alice's dormitory, and a long, wooden table for meals in the middle. Although men and women were separated on this deck, Tom, being a young boy, was allowed to stay with his sister, for which Alice was profoundly thankful.

Their luggage stowed, Alice and Tom were acquainted with the rules and regulations for ship-board life; times for provisions, washing, airing of bedding and daily cleaning of the berths. To Alice, it all sounded eminently sensible. She was used to living in cramped conditions and knew that orderly tidiness could vastly improve the sanitary quality of life.

On deck, they watched the River

Thames widen into the open sea, and then later saw the southern coastline slip past until it became too dark to see anything except the winking lights of Dover and the Channel ports.

It was strange to have supper in the dimly-lit room with a dozen strangers, but everyone was very friendly, and the women made a great fuss of Tom. It was stranger still to sleep in the narrow, wooden bunk, and to feel the gentle heaving motion of the sea beneath them. The engine noise was distracting, but Alice was tired after the early start and excitement of the day, and fell asleep almost at once.

It didn't take them long to slip into the daily routine of life on the SS Pathan. After a few days, it was second nature to sweep and clean the berths every morning, breakfast with the others at the long, central table, and take the bedding out to air on the decks. Alice made a point of doing this daily, although she noticed some women tackled the chore on a very casual basis, in spite of the steward's warning that infestation of all sorts would occur unless they were scrupulous about hygiene.

In the beginning, the weather was kind, the sea calm, and Alice enjoyed the fresh air and sea breezes as the ship steamed out towards the Atlantic Ocean. On the third day, she and Tom were shaking mattresses outside on the lower deck when a resonant voice bade them, 'Good-morning.'

Turning, she saw the man she'd taken to be Jim on the day of embarkation, leaning back against the rails watching them. He was hatless, and the light wind ruffled his dark hair: His tanned face was strong featured, with a long nose and well-shaped mouth.

'Out early with the bedding I see.' He spoke pleasantly, with a light, unfamiliar accent which she took to be Australian.

'Yes. The steward told us it was important.'

'So it is. Bed bugs and lice can cause havoc on a long voyage.' He came away from the rail and looked more closely at her. 'You're the young lady on the pier. You looked as though you knew me.'

Alice bit her lip in annoyance. What a fool he must have taken her for.

'I'm sorry. For a brief moment, I thought you were someone else. That's all. Come, Tom, we must finish tidying the berths.'

The man put out a hand to detain her. 'Just a minute. The berths won't disappear. If we're to be travelling companions we must introduce ourselves. I'm Ned McCartney, travelling from London to Fremantle.'

His blue-eyed smile was so open and friendly, Alice's reserve melted. She'd read that Australians weren't as formal as the English. If she was going to live there it'd be as well to get used to it. She put out her hand.

'Alice Foster, travelling from London to Fremantle with my brother, Tom.'

His grip was warm and firm. 'Pleased

47

to know you. And you, Tom. I imagine you're taking good care of your sister on the voyage.'

'Yes, sir!' Tom took an immediate liking to the tall stranger.

'Would you care to stroll about the deck, Miss Alice and Tom?' Ned asked.

'Oh, no, thank you. We must take these sheets back — and we're lower deck passengers.'

'So?' Ned frowned.

'I believe we keep to our own decks, do we not?'

'Stuff and nonsense,' he snorted. 'You'll find the captain, a Fremantle man, has democratic views — though he's a stickler for discipline. In any case, I'm free to wander the entire ship at will.'

Alice's brown eyes widened, then she cloaked them with thick-fringed lashes. He was very sure of himself! And very good looking! She wondered about Tilly, the girl he'd left behind in London. Natural curiosity made her want to accept his offer, but pride and modesty declined.

'I'm fully occupied today, Mr McCartney. As you see, I have my brother to attend to.'

Stifling Tom's protests by throwing the sheets over his shoulders, she nodded graciously and swept away down the deck.

Ned called after her. 'To the next morning of the bed sheets then, Miss Foster.'

His deep laugh rang in her ears all the way back to the lower-deck cabins.

3

Alice and Tom enjoyed the shipboard life; the weather continued kind, with calm seas and blue skies. A camaraderie developed amongst the lower deck passengers. There was always plenty to do and, to Alice, it felt like the holiday she'd never had. Tom made friends with other children, so she was often free to stroll the deck and talk to the other women.

Often, as she shook and aired their bedding, Ned McCartney would come by and stop to talk. He invariably asked her to take a walk on the upper decks with him, but each time she declined. She learned, from one of the women, that Ned was the ship's surgeon, and his tour of the lower deck was part of his duty.

The woman said how wonderfully kind he'd been to her small daughter who'd developed a high fever, and been fearful sea-sick, too. When Ned spoke, he'd volunteered little information about himself, their exchanges being confined to the weather and the ship's progress.

It was in the Bay of Biscay that the weather began to change. The seas ran high, and the ship began to pitch and roll. Most passengers disappeared from the decks, suffering sea-sickness in their cabins below. Alice was delighted to find that neither she nor Tom suffered in the slightest from the heaving of the ship. On the contrary, she found the crashing seas exhilarating, and loved to be out on the deck to watch them.

The ship was about to turn at the southernmost point of Spain when suddenly a huge wave rolled the ship almost horizontal. Everything on the deck that wasn't fastened down slid about freely. Alice was taken completely by surprise. The few hardy passengers around went sprawling across the slippery, wet decks, grabbing for a hold on anything which was stationary.

Alice hooked one arm around a stout rail and grasped Tom with the other, but his coat sleeve slipped through her fingers and he, too, went flying across the unstable deck, only crashing to a halt against a heavy, iron stanchion.

'Tom,' she yelled, 'don't move. Hang on.' She could see he was hurt. He lay gasping, clutching his leg, his face furrowed in pain.

The ship rolled upright slowly, dipped a little into the next wave, then continued its regular up and down pitching movement.

'A freak wave,' someone said.

One of the sailors on deck, assisting the passengers who'd fallen, added, 'We caught the swell and the wind as we turned the point. It'll calm down from now on. Anyone hurt here?'

'My brother — over there.' Alice rushed over to where Tom lay.

'You all right, lad? Can you get up?' The seaman kneeled down and tried to move him gently.

'Aaargh! My leg — it hurts.'

'Right. You stay there. I'll get the doctor as fast as possible. Seems like everyone else is all right. Just stay here, miss, with your brother, I'll get some help. Looks like that leg's had a bad knock.' He gestured one of the women standing nearby to help, then ran off.

'Poor lad.' The woman brought a folded shawl and put it under Tom's head. 'Lucky more of us weren't injured. It's much calmer now.'

The ship had moved into the lee of the land and the huge waves had miraculously lessened. More people came out on deck to see what had happened, and to sympathise with Alice and Tom. One young man, who claimed to be a medical student, felt the length of Tom's injured leg gingerly, hazarding a guess that no bones were broken. A crowd gathered round, and Alice began to fear that Tom would faint from pain and lack of air.

'Please, move back a little,' she

pleaded, but this was such an interesting diversion in the ship's routine, people were loth to move away and, naturally, they all had advice to offer!

'Get him some water. He's as pale as death.'

'And for the girl, too. She looks a bit white.'

'Something stronger'd be better.' A flask was proffered and a strong smell of spirits made Tom gag.

'Please!' Alice repeated in desperation as the crowd pressed even closer. A dark stain from Tom's leg began to ooze along the deck.

'Cup of tea'll be best. Who'll go and make one?'

Then, as if by magic, the crowd parted and dissolved as a tall figure cut a swathe through the onlookers.

A sharp, authoritarian command rang out. 'Clear a way there. All move back. Do you want to crush the lad?' Ned McCartney strode through the throng, thrusting the curious aside.

'Away,' he repeated, and everyone retreated.

'Miss Foster — and Tom.' His voice was soft as he crouched down beside them both. 'Here's a piece of ill-luck.'

'Is it bad? He's in such pain.' She was so relieved that Ned was there, and Tom looked happier, too.

'Let's have a look, then I'll give you something for the pain. Was it the wave which knocked you off-balance?'

Tom nodded. 'I — wasn't quick enough. I'm sorry.'

'Never mind that. How could you know such a sneaky whopper would catch us like that.' Carefully, he examined Tom's leg, his eyes noting the pain reaction as his fingers pressed and probed. He cut away the cloth from Tom's leg cautiously, then covered it quickly before Alice could see. 'No bones broken, but a bad gash. We'll get him to the sick bay.'

'What! What is it?' Alice clutched his arm in fear.

He covered her hand with his. 'Don't

be frightened. Come along with him. I'll get a stretcher. Even if he could stand, I wouldn't want him to put any weight on his leg.'

The Pathan was the newest ship in the Line, and had well-equipped sick bay accommodation on the main deck. The medical student helped carry the stretcher and stayed with Ned as he worked on Tom's injured leg.

Alice couldn't see what they were doing — she'd been ordered to the back of the area, and it seemed an age before Ned moved away from the table. She saw him tuck a blanket around Tom before he scrubbed his hands and put his jacket on again.

He nodded to the student. 'Thanks. Glad you were here. Can you keep an eye on Tom for a few minutes? I want to talk to Miss Foster.'

'Be glad to. You did a good job there, sir.'

'Hope so. We won't know for a while. I'll be back shortly.'

Alice moved towards the bunk where

Tom lay, his eyes closed. 'Can't I stay here? What's wrong with his leg? Why did you put him to sleep?'

'I had to stitch the leg. Come up on deck, Alice. I want to talk to you.' He took her arm and steered her into the corridor. 'Tom'll be all right alone for a minute or two.'

She allowed herself to be led up on deck. Ned's grip was tight on her elbow, and she was amazed to see that it was almost dark.

'It's been hours. I didn't realise.'

'Tom's leg is quite bad. Look, there're seats over there. You'd better sit down. I don't want another invalid on my hands.'

'It's just a bad knock — surely.'

'A bit more serious. I'm afraid he's ruptured an artery. No — sit down. Let me tell you — '

'That sounds terrible. What does it mean?'

'At best — a few days in bed. He's lost a lot of blood, and he needs rest, but if the artery doesn't mend — '

'Will it? Is that what you were doing — stitching it?'

'Yes. It should mend all right. He's young and healthy — '

'If not?' she demanded.

Ned paused, then took both her hands in his. 'I have to tell you, Alice — I hope it won't be necessary, but if the artery doesn't hold, then the blood flow to the leg will go — and — I may — I may have to amputate the foot.'

'Oh, no! Please, please don't do that. Poor Tom. And it's all my fault.'

'Of course it's not — and I've told you, he has a good chance. I had to warn you, but you mustn't say anything to Tom. He must be absolutely still and quiet. It'll be up to you to nurse him. I'll arrange for him to stay in the sick bay, and you, too.'

'I can't. We haven't the money. We're lower-deck passengers.'

Ned looked grim. 'If you move him, he most certainly will lose the foot.'

'Then he must stay, whatever the cost.'

'Good girl. Let me worry about the money. You just look after your brother. Now, we'll get back to him, and pray we have calm seas for a while, too.'

For forty-eight hours Alice never left her brother's bedside. Under Ned's instructions, she fed and washed Tom, tended the wound, and made sure he moved as little as possible. Having done its damage, the sea was tranquil, but at the least rolling motion, she held his body still with her own, willing the artery to heal, praying he would keep his limbs whole.

On the third day, Ned examined the leg, and smiled at Alice's anxious look.

'It's going to be fine. The artery's healing.'

'Thank God. Oh, thank God.' She flung her arms around Ned's neck. 'And thank you.'

He held her against his chest, felt her heart beating, and put his own arms round her.

With a sigh, she settled against him, feeling his strength and power, the physician's power, which had healed her brother. Warmth spread through her tired body, and she felt she could stay in the comfort of the doctor's arms for ever. Ned stroked her thick hair.

'You've been an excellent nurse. Pity there aren't more patients. You should rest now. You haven't slept in two days.'

'Tom's slept enough for both of us!'

'I had to keep him well sedated, but he'll be fully awake soon, and then you'll have your hands full. He'll be lively, and bored, but he still mustn't move much. Come up on deck with me for a breath of air — then sleep.'

'Can I stay here — by Tom?'

'Of course — if you'll take a walk with me now.'

The ship had travelled through the Straits of Gibraltar, and much of the Mediterranean. It was a warm night, with brighter stars than Alice had ever seen. She looked up at the velvet-gemmed night and said a prayer of thanks that Tom hadn't been crippled. Full of gratitude to Ned, she breathed in the night air deeply, glad to be free of the odours of the sick bay.

Ned watched her face, upturned to the silver moon. 'Just you and Tom in the world? You're very young to be travelling so far on your own.'

'I'm nearly twenty — and I've got lots of family: Dad, three brothers and a sister. They're to join us soon.'

'And where's that to be?'

'I'm not sure exactly.' Ned's eyebrows rose, and Alice added quickly, 'I'm to be met in Fremantle, and I have an address near a place called Northam.'

Ned looked surprised. 'Northam! That's very near to where I live.'

'Really?' It was Alice's turn to look astonished. 'But aren't you a ship's doctor?'

Ned laughed. 'Only temporarily. I am a doctor — I've been to Edinburgh doing research, but my family has a cattle ranch near Northam. I'm going to have a spell helping out for a while, but I shall keep my hand in medicine, too. The area's very short of medical facilities. I'd like to start a small hospital.'

'What a coincidence that we should both be going to the same area.'

'Not really. There are few enough people out there yet. I'd bet that half the settlers on this boat'll be your nearish neighbours eventually. Don't you know the name of the place you're going to?'

'I'll know when I'm met at Fremantle, though I'm to contact the Crossley Ranch — if my — if — I — the person who should meet me isn't there.'

For some reason Alice baulked at mentioning Jim, but Ned's dark brows were drawn into a frown.

'The Crossleys? Why would you be going there? It's — ' He stopped abruptly — he didn't want to alarm Alice. She'd had enough to worry about since Tom's accident. In the white moonlight, she looked enchantingly ethereal. He wondered if she had any idea about life in the vast new country. 'Do you know the Crossleys then?' he probed.

'No, it's just an address my — my — ' Why couldn't she say fiancé? ' — my friend gave me, in case of emergencies.'

Ned hesitated to say that it would be more likely she'd run into the emergencies at the Crossley household.

'So, who is this friend who's meeting you in Fremantle, and what connection does she, or he, have with the Crossleys?'

It was no use hedging any longer, and there was no reason anyway. She said with a rush, 'I'm going to be married in Fremantle. My — friend — Jim Peterson wrote home telling us what a fine place Western Australia is. He had a hard time for the first four years, then he struck gold in Kalgoorlie. He sent out money for me — second-class cabin, but I brought Tom along instead, transferring to the lower deck. And the rest of the family's to follow, as soon as

Jim can find a place for us all.'

'Married — but you must have been very young when your fiancé left England.' He thought she looked no more than a slip of a youngster now.

He had been standing very close to her, their shoulders almost touching, but as he spoke, she felt him move away, putting distance between them.

'Do you know the Crossley Ranch?' she asked, sensing a reticence in him.

For a while he didn't speak, then he said slowly, as though weighing each word, 'Our homestead, the McCartneys, is practically adjacent to the Crossleys. But you say this is just an emergency address?'

'Yes — if Jim's not able to meet me off the ship, but I'm to go to the P & O Hotel in Fremantle.'

'Well then, it's unlikely you'll be going to the Crossley's, so it doesn't matter. No doubt your Jim will have a fine house in Fremantle for you, if he's done as well as he says.'

'But he's buying land to grow wheat

and fruit. Farming — work for all my family. It'll be a wonderful life, a new start for all of us.'

Ned leaned on the deck rail, looking out over the moonlit sea. He avoided Alice's eyes.

'I'm sure it will be.' Sombrely, he added quietly, 'I sincerely hope so.'

Soon after the conversation with Ned, Alice went back to the lower deck quarters, and a few days later, Tom left the sick bay. He had to be careful and keep his foot rested, but now he no longer needed nursing care there were plenty of women to spoil and tend to him.

The days and weeks went by. The Pathan steamed its way through the Suez Canal, the Red Sea, and well into the Indian Ocean. The suffocating heat knocked out more passengers than the freak wave which had so nearly crippled Tom. Even at night it was too hot to sleep, and many passengers simply lay out on deck, waiting patiently for a cooling breeze.

Alice had seen little of Ned since Tom left the sick bay. Unconsciously, she looked for his tall figure when she was airing the bedding, but apart from the occasional distant glimpse as he toured the lower deck on his medical round, he did not approach her. She missed his easy presence and strength, but told herself he must be busy with patients for, as the voyage progressed, more people fell ill, mostly as a result of the oppressive heat. Two people died; one of fever, another, older woman, simply expired, as if in despair of ever reaching her destination.

Then, one day, Ned sought out Alice, asking her to help him in the sick bay. The babies on the ship were suffering in the heat, and their mothers, frequently with other children to tend, were unable to cope. She gladly helped Ned cool down the infants, bathing them with chilled flannels, soothing their restlessness.

'You're an instinctive nurse,' he said to her one day. 'I saw that when you were looking after Tom. You could do nursing training. There's a great need for good nurses.'

'But I'll be busy on the land. Jim has promised — everything's going to be fine.'

'Have you known — Jim — long? Back in London?'

'All my early life. We grew up together, then he left . . . and . . . ' She tailed off.

'And,' Ned prompted, 'he wrote letters, telling you all about the place.'

'Er . . . yes.' Alice hated to lie, but she felt she should be protective towards Jim, and anyway, it was none of Ned McCartney's business. She wondered how she could ask him about Tilly.

In the Indian Ocean, with nothing between the ship and the vast Australian continent, sea breezes began to assuage the discomfort and the fevers. People began to talk of arriving there, plans were discussed, descriptions of the friends and relatives who were to be at the dockside were exchanged.

Alice continued to help Ned when needed, but as the voyage neared its end, the health of the passengers improved dramatically, as though, having come all this way, and so near journey's end, they couldn't afford to be less than one hundred percent fit to cope with their next adventure. Alice sensed Ned wanted to tell her something; there was a holding back, and a speculative look in his eye that made her uneasy.

As they neared the West Coast of Australia, a storm blew up like a final test and tribulation. The passengers were driven below deck, and many suffered sea-sickness again. Worse still, the ship was running short of coal, and could not enter Fremantle's difficult harbour because of the high seas. The captain posted bulletins on the ship's notice-boards regretting the delay, and informing passengers that the ship would make a run for Albany, a little farther down the coast. There, they could enter the safer harbour, refuel and return to Fremantle.

Alice was probably the only person to be secretly delighted by the news; apart from her worry over Tom's injury, she'd loved every minute of the voyage. Though, of course, she was looking forward to seeing Jim.

Ninety-three days after setting out from London, the SS Pathan entered the lovely natural harbour of Albany. Alice and Tom were on deck early in the morning for their first glimpse of Australian life.

'Can we go ashore, Alice? Please.' Tom hopped about with excitement. 'Look — the beaches. The sand's snow white. It's beautiful.'

Indeed it was. The harbour, apart from a small, rocky opening, was encircled by a belt of woodland. Two wooden piers thrust into the water, and the granite hills behind were clothed in very tall trees. A handful of houses fringed the gently sloping hill behind the water.

Alice laughed at her brother's enthusiasm.

'I think we can go — for a while. We're not leaving until tonight. Let's set our feet on Australian soil. A launch is coming for those who want to go ashore.'

They wandered through the main street of Albany, a sleepy port with a general store, bakery and small hotel. Alice was enchanted — if this was Australia, she was going to love it. After London's East End, it was idyllic. Open spaces, clean air and the sea.

The cakes in the bakery looked deliciously fresh. Tom pressed his nose against the glass panes. Alice said indulgently, 'Choose which you want. Fresh baked will be a treat.'

A familiar voice turned her head. 'Alice, Tom, welcome to Australia. Allow me to escort you round my home town.' Ned McCartney, hatless, casually dressed in a loose shirt and seaman's trousers, stood behind them.

'Albany — your home town? I

thought — ' Alice began.

'I was born here. My parents bought land north of here when I was a youngster, so we moved out to establish the ranch. I'm about to visit my favourite aunt. Do join me. She'll be delighted to meet folk from the old country.'

'Oh — we couldn't intrude.'

'Don't be so — so English! You'll meet with much more informality here, and hospitality, so you'd better make a start right now. My arm, Miss Foster. Come, Tom.' His smile was attractive.

The small town, with the open landscape behind, seemed a fitting backcloth for Ned. He epitomised the new order of things — clean-cut, powerful, an outdoor kind of man! Alice took his arm. Tom put his hand into Ned's free one.

Miss Nellie McCartney was over-joyed to see her nephew, and full of warm welcome for his English companions. Sandwiches, cakes and tea appeared in a flash, and Nellie had the story of the voyage and Alice's family out of her in no time. Her one-storey house looked directly on to King George's Sound, and Alice fell in love with the place immediately. The time flew by, and Ned had to remind them they must be getting back to the ship.

'Can't you stay a little longer? It's so nice to have company,' Nellie pleaded.

' 'Fraid not this time, Auntie. It'd never do for Alice to miss the boat. She's looking forward to meeting her fiancé at long last.'

'He'll be in Fremantle, you say?' Nellie was putting the remains of the tea into a bag for them to take back to the ship.

'I hope so. If not, I've to go to the Crossley ranch, near Northam.'

A plate slipped out of Nellie's hand — scones tumbled to the floor. She bent to retrieve them, but not before Alice had glimpsed surprised alarm in her face as she glanced across to her nephew.

She straightened up and said firmly,

'Before you go, Alice, you must see my pride and joy. I've had a new bath-house built in the back. Do use it, and tell me what you think. You, too, Tom.'

Alice stood up and obediently went along to the room Nellie showed her. When she and Tom returned, Aunt Nellie and Ned were in earnest discussion.

'Ned, you must warn her. She can't possibly go to the Crossley place, especially since Eva went.'

'I can't do that. In any case, her fiancé will meet her in Fremantle — and it's not my business — she's going to be married. Don't worry, Auntie, I'm sure she'll be all right. She's a sensible sort of girl, and I believe — ' He broke off as Alice came into the room.

Alice hadn't wanted to hear any more. 'It's a lovely washroom,' she said brightly. 'I was tempted to have a bath in that tub.'

'Another day, I hope.' Aunt Nellie

73

fussed around Tom. 'You'll come and visit me when you're settled down?'

'If we're not too far away, I'd love it.'

Alice and Tom said their goodbyes, and went outside whilst Ned bade his own farewell. The bright sunshine lifted Alice's spirits, which had been depressed by what she'd heard.

She grabbed Tom's hand. 'Come on. Mr McCartney'll follow us.'

All these hints about the Crossley place! It didn't matter because they wouldn't be going there. Anyway, it couldn't be as bad as the dreadful harshness of their life in London. Alice was, as ever, a determined optimist.

4

In moderate seas, refuelled, and with a following wind, the SS Pathan made good speed back up the coast to Fremantle.

Now journey's end was finally in sight, there was hectic activity in cabins and below decks. Possessions were bundled together; bedding shaken out and rolled up for the last time. Those passengers with friends or relatives to meet them were eager to be away and off the ship. Others, the government sponsored immigrants, were apprehensive, wondering what might lie ahead. They were the ones who lingered below, saying their goodbyes to shipboard friends, promising to keep in touch, if possible. Ned had been right, a number of Alice's travelling companions were to settle in the lands beyond Fremantle.

Alice and Tom were to be met, so they were among the first to claim a place at the harbourside rails as the ship steamed into port. Fremantle was larger, by far, than Albany, though smaller than London. Stone jetties jutted from the quayside, and large sheds lined the dock. Behind the harbour, tall, stone buildings told of a rapidly-growing town.

As the Pathan juddered and came to rest against the wooden dockside, they could see, waiting below, eager, upturned faces scanning the passengers lining the rails. Alice and Tom, at the rail, could feel the weight of people becoming heavy behind them. Just as she thought she must extricate Tom from the press, she suddenly found breathing easier. Turning, she found them both protected from behind by the broad chest and shoulders of Ned McCartney.

He was laughing, dark eyes full of excitement. He gestured around the harbour. 'Isn't it a fine sight? It's a great place — you'll be happy here.'

Alice caught his mood and smiled. 'I hope so — I'm sure so.' Shyly she asked, 'You're glad to be home?'

'Of course. Travelling's good, but home is where we all belong. Never fear, Alice, you'll come to love Australia — you and your young man. I'll be glad to meet him, once you're settled.'

'Have you — will you have someone down there to meet you?' She avoided the thought of Jim and Ned together. Somehow it wouldn't gel in her mind.

'I expect so. The McCartney's are quite a clan. I've a lot of family in Perth, too. They're sure to have made the trip to see the prodigal return.'

The crowd below pressed forward against the restraints of harbour and customs' officials, who would be first on board, to instigate immigration procedures.

Tom stretched up on tip-toe, pulling at Alice's sleeve. 'Can you see Jim in the crowd?'

She craned forward. 'No, not yet, but

there are more people over by the sheds. They're too far away to recognise.' She daren't voice a lurking fear that she just might not recognise Jim!

'I can't see him either.' Tom sounded doubtful.

'I'm not surprised. You were only five years old when he left London.'

'I shall remember him though.' Tom was stubborn.

The gang planks rattled down and officials started to board. Disembarkation began and passengers began to move away from the rails.

Ned was separated from them, but he waved and called out, 'I'll see you on the quay — to say goodbye.'

Alice eyed the milling crowd and doubted they would find each other again. It looked chaotic, but eventually the passengers were processed. Tom and Alice found themselves once more on the solid ground of Australia. The press of people was great, and she clutched her brother tightly to her side, frightened that he might be swept away from her on the tide of humanity thronging the quay.

Immigrants with no clear destinations were shepherded into vast sheds, a queue snaking back along the walls. They couldn't all be dealt with in one day, and many would be housed in sheds nearby, or even sent back aboard the ship until they could be sorted out. Those who were met by friends or relatives clogged up the dockside, making a party of the welcome home. Alice watched many reunions, pushing away any tremor of unease. There was no sign of Jim Peterson, but she wasn't tall, and she and Tom were lost in the crush. Once it cleared, Jim would find them.

At least the tall figure shouldering his way towards them was familiar. She'd noticed Ned was one of the last to leave the ship, with the other officers. As soon as his feet touched land, he'd been enveloped by at least a dozen people of assorted ages and sizes. Each in turn had been swept into a whirling delighted embrace. Then she'd lost sight of him as she moved luggage and Tom a little apart from the main crowd to make it easier for Jim to spot them.

Ned had detached himself from his welcoming party, though Alice could see them in the distance laughing and chattering, one or two casting curious glances back to Ned, who swept off his hat, taking Alice's hand.

'Alice — and Tom. I've come to say goodbye.' He frowned. 'Is there no sign of Jim Peterson?'

'Not yet, but he'll be here soon. There are so many people . . . '

Head and shoulders above the crowd, Ned's glance raked round. 'What's he look like? Can I help you find him?'

'No! No, please. Look, your friends are calling. We'll be all right. He warned me he might be delayed and, don't forget, the ship's behind schedule because we had to go to Albany first.'

'He'd have found that out from the shipping office here. Surely he'd have waited?'

'Ned, the carriage is here. Come along.' A tall, handsome woman called and beckoned impatiently across the multitude of heads.

'Please — do go,' Alice said desperately. The longer he stayed, the more unsettled she felt. 'I'd rather you weren't here when Jim arrives,' she cried out.

At the same time, the woman called out again. 'Ne-ed. Do come.'

He stared down at Alice, dark eyes concerned, but he dropped her hand and bent to shake hands with Tom. He put a square of card in the boy's pocket.

'Tom, I know you'll look after your sister, but if you need help at any time, the address on this card will find me. Memorise it, in case you lose it.' He stood up. 'Alice, you remember, too, I'm not too far away, and if Jim doesn't come today, go to the P & O Hotel. There may be a message, and you can wait there.'

'I know,' she said coolly. 'Jim's

arranged all that.'

His eyes lingered on her face, but she drew herself up proudly, and he shrugged, bowed and turned to go back to his party. To the wheeling gulls above he muttered, 'I sincerely hope he has arranged all that.'

His broad back was lost and, as his relatives received him back in their midst, a hollow feeling lodged in the pit of Alice's stomach. It belied the proud hauteur with which she'd rebuffed his offer of help, but he had his own family, and Jim would surely come soon.

Tom silently took out the card, read it, mouthed the words on it several times, then put it back in his pocket. The address, strange though it was compared to his own in London, was firmly fixed in his brain.

Hours later, the dockside crowds had dispersed, the queues had dwindled, and still no-one had claimed the two figures sitting forlornly on the tin trunk. Twice, officials had gestured them to join the queue of immigrants, but each time Alice had shaken her head. The third time, she had to produce Jim's letter, and shown that she had money with her.

'Well, you can't stay here much longer, miss. We're about to close up. I should do as this Jim Peterson says, and go to the P & O Hotel. He's obviously been delayed. It happens sometimes.'

'Can't we wait just a little longer? I'm sure he'll come soon.'

The officer looked doubtful, but Alice's large, brown eyes touched a soft spot. 'Tell you what — there's a tea wagon over there. Run along, laddie, tell them I said to give you two cups of tea, and a bun if there's any left. Then, if your man's still not here, you can get a carriage to town, and go to the P & O Hotel. It's only a few hundred yards up the main street.'

The hot tea and buns cheered them both. Alice was disappointed, but Jim had warned this might happen. She refused to consider that his absence was for any reason other than a missed train, or urgent business connected with his land purchase or gold strike. She'd studied the geography of Western Australia from the public library map back home and knew that the distance between settlements was vast, and the railway network very new.

At dusk, the Customs sheds began to close. Still no Jim! There was nothing else for it — he'd said to go to the P & O Hotel, and as everyone else seemed determined to get her there, that's where they'd go.

'Tom, you look after the trunk. I'll get a carriage. It'll be fun to drive to town.'

'Isn't Jim coming then?' Tom fingered the card in his pocket. 'What about Ned? Couldn't we go to his house?'

'Of course not! I expect he and his family'll be going to Perth before going out to their farm, and in any case, we're here to meet Jim.'

She stiffened her back, tied her bonnet strings more firmly, and went to summon a horse cabbie.

The Pacific and Orient Hotel, built by the steamship company for the convenience of its officers and cabin-class passengers, was a grand, Victorian building of local honey-coloured limestone.

Alice refused to be intimidated by its ornate façade, and marched into the reception area as though daily in and out of the best hotels in London. It helped that she was wearing her only bit of finery, a new, pearl-grey, silk gown, and pink trimmed bonnet to match. She'd made it herself, buying the material out of Jim's money. She'd hoped to do him proud by wearing it for their first meeting.

It impressed the desk manager, whose eyes brightened with admiration as she enquired for any messages for Miss Alice Foster, from London, England, just arrived on the SS Pathan. If he thought it strange to be dealing with a young, unaccompanied girl and small boy, he didn't show it. Indeed, in this new, but growing, port town, he was used to dealing with strange situations.

He looked along the rack of letters. 'No, miss. There's nothing for you. Were you expecting someone?'

Alice hid her disappointment. 'May we wait here? I'm expecting my — friend at any time.'

It was already dark outside, and the man looked dubious. 'It's getting late. I wouldn't advise you to go out again. If your friend doesn't arrive, we do have rooms upstairs. You and the young gentleman could surely share for the night. Would you require dinner?' He mentioned the cost discreetly.

Alice swallowed her shock, agreed it was best to reserve a room for Tim and herself, but refused dinner. Later, they could stroll the streets, buy bread and fruit and eat in their rooms.

Upstairs, there was hot, running water, snowy bath linen, and a fat cake of soap. To Alice and Tom it was luxury undreamed of, and with youthful optimism, they enjoyed the pleasures, pushing away thoughts of the morrow. It was clear Jim wasn't coming that night.

Tom, worn out by the strange novelties of the day, soon fell asleep. Alice sat a while by the window, listening to the night sounds from the street below, but soon she, too, started to yawn. In spite of her anxieties, the soft, feather mattress sucked her into deep sleep, and for some hours both she and Tom were blissfully oblivious of what lay before them.

★ ★ ★

The streets and bars of Fremantle, being a port town, remained lively into the early hours. Sailors, mining prospectors and farmers from the outlying districts, in town for supplies, all drank together. The P & O Hotel rooms were dark and quiet, but the public bar was raucous with the noise of hard-drinking men. There were no women of repute there.

The man who arrived at midnight and asked the barman if a Miss Alice Foster was in the hotel was rough and unkempt, his clothes stained and dusty. The barman hesitated, and the man growled impatiently.

'I don't want to see her. There's a message.'

'Write it down. Can't you see I'm busy?'

'Can't write. Just tell 'er, him she's come to see — he'll be at Crossley's, and to take the train to Northam. She'll be met.'

'What train?' The barman was preoccupied.

'How should I know? Mebbe there's only one. Just pass on the message and give me some beer.' He'd done as asked. For what he'd been paid, he wouldn't have bothered, but he was staying over in Fremantle, and he liked the P & O bar. He picked up the pint pot and drank thirstily, the name of

Alice Foster already forgotten . . .

The man behind the desk frowned at the scrap of paper and passed it to Alice the next morning. He had a young daughter, and hated to think of Alice alone in this town with only a young boy as companion.

'Mick, the barman, must have left it last night,' he volunteered.

'But who brought it? There's no name.' Alice had been excited when she'd been told there was a message, fully expecting it to be a telegraph from Jim saying when he was arriving. She picked up the note. It was ill-written — barely legible. 'Can I see the barman? The man who took it.'

'He only works nights here. I suppose you could wait until this evening.'

Alice rubbed her cheek and thought for a while. She was tired of waiting around. Jim had obviously been delayed. Now, any sort of action would be preferable. 'No. We'll go to Northam. How far is it?'

'Not far — hundred miles or so.

There's only the one train — noon, from Perth. Cobb's Coaches'll take you to the station. I can fix it if you want.'

'Please — and do you know exactly where Crossley's Ranch is?'

The man blinked. 'Frank Crossley's place? Is that where you're going?'

'Yes. I'm to meet my fiancé there. Do you know it?'

The man looked away. He was sorry for the young pair, but it was none of his business. At least it couldn't have been Frank himself who'd delivered the message. Mick, the barman, knew Frank, who was well known in all the town's ale houses — or used to be, in the old days. But if Miss Foster was meeting her young man — surely that'd be all right.

'I know of it,' he replied cautiously. 'Your friend'll be there?'

'Oh, yes, certain to be,' Alice said brightly.

The man's conscience pricked. To assuage it he said, 'Why don't you have breakfast while I see about your luggage, and the train?'

Alice mentally totted up her money. Just enough for the coach, train and food. They'd spent more than she'd intended, but she'd soon be seeing Jim. Recklessly, she took her brother's hand.

'Why not? I'm quite hungry. You must be, too, Tom.' She refused to wonder why Jim hadn't come himself — there had to be some simple explanation, and at least, he'd got a message to her.

The desk clerk himself took them to the dining-room, saw them seated, then took the waiter aside.

'Look after those two young 'uns. Make sure they have a good breakfast.'

It was an instinctive act of charity, based on a shadowy notion that, if things didn't turn out well, at least the travellers would be well fed. He didn't like what he'd heard about the Crossley Ranch, and thanked his lucky stars that it wasn't his daughter going there.

5

Alice had never been on a train before. She'd seen them in London, read about them, and imagined how exciting it would be to ride in one. Now she wasn't too sure!

The August day, towards the winter's end in Western Australia, was hot, the air in the carriage stifling. Tom had opened the windows but, as the train jerked its way along the track, steam, smoke and hot cinders blew in, making the air even more difficult to breathe. No-one else had boarded their carriage at Perth, so she and Tom were able to exclaim aloud their amazement at the scenery; red earth and olive scrub — so different from the fields around London.

The train stopped frequently on the track for no apparent reason, and it was an hour before they arrived at the first official stop, Midland, where there were more passengers to board.

Alice was a little alarmed when two dirty, bewhiskered men clambered up the steps. They smelled strongly of beer, and their leery glances at her made Tom sit up as tall as he could. He fastened his eyes on the men, daring them to say anything. Alice put a warning hand on his arm, wondering if it would be cowardly to change carriages, but no, this was a rough country, and there was no reason to think the men would harm her. Nevertheless, she was relieved when a solid-looking, middle-aged woman came to sit by her, giving her a friendly nod.

'Nearly missed the train again.' She pointed to her empty wicker baskets. 'Eggs went good at the market today. Sold out!' She peered curiously at Alice and Tom. 'Didn't see you there. Strangers, are you?' The accent was similar to Ned's.

'Yes — I — we've only been in Australia a short while.'

'Aha! English I'd say. From London? Got relatives there myself.'

She smiled even more broadly, and Alice felt much more at home for the tenuous link. The woman chattered on about her relatives, and told Alice that she and her husband had a small farm a few miles out of Midland, where she'd been to sell produce, and buy supplies.

One of the men took out a flask, swigged from it, and with a smirk, leaned forward and offered it to Alice. She shrank back.

The woman struck his hand away sharply. 'You mind your manners. Is it likely she'll be wanting to drink that after you?'

'You mind your business, missus.' The man scowled, but sat back and passed the flask to his companion.

'Thank you though.' Alice, confused, mindful of her position, didn't want to offend anyone.

'Don't you be thanking him — he'll not need encouraging. Both of 'em have had too much as it is.'

Alice was impressed by the severe look she shot at them, and vowed to practise one of her own! It seemed to quell both men, although they continued to pass the flask to one another.

The woman concentrated her attention on the interesting newcomers.

'And where ye heading dear — with the young 'un?'

'This is my brother, Tom. We're going to Northam — the Crossley place.' She said it half-fearfully and, of course, reaction was instantaneous. Both men, goggle-eyed, paused, bottle midway between them. The woman drew breath sharply.

'Crossley's! What . . . ?'

'Don't look the usual type to me.'

'Lucky devil, Frank.'

The comments were simultaneous, and one of the men half rose in his seat, as though to sit by Alice.

The woman stopped him. 'Hush your mouth — and get back there.' To Alice, she said softly, 'And why would you be going out there — you and the boy?'

'I'm going to meet my fiancé — Jim Peterson. Do you know of him, or this Mr Crossley?'

The older woman spoke hesitantly. 'Can't say I do know a Jim Peterson, though I did hear Frank Crossley had hired help. That was some time ago, but now . . . ' She tailed off, settled her shawl firmly round her broad shoulders, and added decisively, 'Still, if your fiancé's there, that'll be all right. I wish you happiness. Maybe we'll meet again if you're to settle in these parts — you and your young man, that is. Here's my stop. Engine driver knows where to put me down.'

She picked up her wicker baskets, turned and glared ferociously at the two men. 'And you'll be leaving these people be. I'll remember your faces again.' To Alice she said, 'Sarah Winthrop's my name. Northam's an hour or so on. Be dark by the time you get there at this rate, but watch out for a lantern. Your young man'll be meeting you, no doubt, and he'll stop the train just short of the town. The Crossley place's a mile or so before. I'll mention it to the guard — and tell him to keep an eye out for these drunken ruffians. Best of luck to you and the youngster.'

'Shan't touch the likes of 'er — especially if she's bound for Crossley's.'

The parting shot was muffled as the woman opened the door and climbed down on to the track. Tom helped to hand down her baskets, and he and Alice waved to her as the train rumbled off. A horse and trap came up to meet her, and the woman turned away with a final wave.

Alice pulled up the window, settled back in her seat, and tried to push away her rising alarm and sense of dejection at being left with the two evil-smelling men, wishing she'd had the courage to follow Sarah and move down the train. But, cowed by the fearsome threats, and now very fuddled by drink, the two men slumped in their seats and fell asleep, snoring thickly.

As dusk gathered, Tom's arm crept through Alice's, and she pressed it tightly, willing the train on — to the safety of Jim Peterson. Whatever was at the Crossley Ranch, she was sure he would stand between it and them.

After about an hour, one of the men awoke on a spluttering, choking breath looked into the darkness outside, and said roughly, 'We're nearly at Northam. Watch out your side for a swinging light — that'll be he — who'll be meeting you.'

Alice was glad she couldn't see his face. His tone was surly, unfriendly, but she thanked him, and tried to brush the smuts and dust from her clothes. Thank goodness she hadn't travelled in the pearl silk — it'd be black silk by now, whereas her dark navy dress, though hot, still looked fairly presentable.

'Don't thank me,' the man growled, subsiding back into stupor. 'You'll more like live to regret it.' He sniffed the air. 'Storm coming, too.'

Tom leaned out of the window.

'Look, there's a light. And Jim — look — he's swinging a lantern to and fro — up ahead. The train's slowing down. We're there, and there's Jim, too.'

Alice strained her eyes through the night, and saw a dark shape behind the swaying yellow light. It came close as the train creaked, slowed, clattered past the figure, to stop several yards ahead, steam hissing all around it. The figure stepped back out of the steam.

The guard leaned out of his van, calling back, 'All right, miss. Down you get, quick — we're on to Northam now.' He tumbled their trunk out on to the track, and blew a whistle.

Tom scrambled out, took the cases from Alice, who barely had time to follow before the train started off again. He slammed the door shut and took his sister's arm. 'Are we there?'

'Yes. Where's Jim? I can't see . . . '

Darkness pressed all round them, the train lights already dwindling to pinpoints. The ground was rough and stony — no signs of any habitation

— no friendly lights.

'Over there.' Tom pulled her sleeve. 'And there's a horse — I can hear it snorting.'

'Jim?' Alice called out in the direction Tom was pointing. She saw the lantern, which wavered, then came uncertainly towards her. 'Jim! It's me — Alice — and Tom.'

She stepped tentatively over the rough ground, trying to make out the face under the broad-brimmed hat. Surely Jim was taller, or was he stooping to see them?

'Jim?' she called again, feeling a cold bead of fear in the hot night.

She didn't recognise the voice that rasped through the oppressive dark, but she knew one thing — it wasn't the voice of Jim Peterson. It had a coarse, unfamiliar twang.

The lantern was thrust in her face. 'Alice Foster, is it? Who's the other? There was no mention of another.'

Alice put up her hand to shield her eyes from the glare, and saw a man's face, swarthy, dark-bearded, glittering eyes — not Jim.

Tom spoke up, his childish treble cracking to a deeper tone. 'I'm Tom Foster. We're here to meet Jim Peterson. Where is he please?'

'And who the blazes is Tom Foster? I'm . . . '

A sudden flash of lightning lit the night sky, outlining the man standing near a horse and cart — the only other thing in sight on the desolate horizon, as far as Alice could see. A violent crack of thunder made her jump, and huge drops of rain spattered her forehead.

'Git along — into the cart,' the voice said. 'You, fellow, pick up the trunk. Put it in the back. Hurry now, there's a downpour to come — '

Alice shouted, 'Leave it, Tom. We're not going with him.' She grabbed the man's arm as he made to turn away. 'Where's my — fiancé, Jim Peterson? Who are you?'

'He can't come. Now you just get in that cart. I'm not standing here all

101

night. The boy needn't come. Nothing was said about a boy — just the girl — you, Alice Foster. It is you, is it?'

'I'm Alice Foster all right, and this is my brother, Tom. He's coming with me. I wrote to Jim about him, but we're not moving a step unless you tell me where Jim is.' The rain was now settling down to a thorough soaking job, the air was steamy, and more thunder crackled.

'You don't have an option, miss. Stay and get drowned then. You're miles from anywhere.'

'Northam's not far away. Could you take us there — to a hotel?'

The raucous laugh underscored the thunder. 'Not on your life. I'm going back home and, if you've any sense, you'll come, too. The rain'll keep up a while, then the track'll be too muddy to go anywhere.'

Tom had already dragged the trunk through the darkness and looked enquiringly up at Alice. He was a pale shadow, hair slicked down with rain. It was a terrible moment of indecision, but she knew she had no choice. In foreign territory, pitch dark and a storm raging, she couldn't risk being left. But the man didn't give her any confidence — a total stranger — tough — unfriendly as the men on the train, but at least he knew her name, and he must have news of Jim. Perhaps Jim was ill and had sent this fellow to pick them up.

As though sensing her indecision, the man said, in a more wheedling tone, 'Look, we're all getting wet. Come along, and I'll tell you about your Jim. You needn't be afraid. I'm Frank Crossley.'

The name almost decided Alice to stay where she was, but Tom took unexpected command. With an almighty effort, he picked up the trunk, heaved it over the side of the cart, and flung in their hand baggage.

'Come on, Alice, we'll have to go with him. Don't worry, I'll look after you.' He took her hand and led her to the cart. 'There's no other way — for now.'

Frank Crossley was already sitting up on the cart, impatiently flicking the reins. He looked back to see the two Fosters huddled together, clutching their bags.

'Go up!' he shouted to the horse, then, whispering into the driving rain, 'Didn't bargain for no boy. That's a spanner in the works, and no mistake.'

The ride was bumpy, rickety, and seemed to last for hours. Alice pulled a rough piece of sacking over them, but they were already soaked through, and the material was soon sodden as well. The cart swayed and jerked along, stopping suddenly from time to time, throwing Tom and Alice against the wooden boards.

Frank's curses floated back to them. 'Danged kangaroos,' he yelled at the shapes which leaped out across the track.

Alice closed her eyes, wondering if and when the nightmare would ever end. SS Pathan, and Ned McCartney, seemed a million days away. She still hoped that Jim would be waiting for them at the Crossley place.

Finally, the horse stopped naturally, not jerked by the reins. It had arrived home.

'Here we are. Leave the trunk. Time enough to see to that in a day or two.'

'I'm not — '

But Frank Crossley had left the cart and horse, and the lantern was already bobbing on ahead, along a slightly less rough track. Alice climbed down stiffly. Tom followed with the bags. She couldn't see a thing. The rain had eased a little; tall trees dripped more wet, there was a dense dark hump ahead, then a square of light, as a piece of sacking was held back.

'In here — hurry in. I've to see to the horse.' Frank Crossley pushed them into a room dimly lit with a paraffin lamp, then disappeared out through the sacking door.

In the poor light, Alice made out a

square room with what looked like wood slabs for walls. A piece of sacking, to match the one serving as a front door, stretched the entire width — she presumed sleeping quarters were behind it. The floor was mud, well tamped down, but dusty and débris strewn. A long wooden table in the centre was covered with plates and mugs, cutlery and bits of food. A dog pawed for scraps, sliding them neatly on to the floor, and with one eye on the newcomers, gulped them down. Rain drummed on an iron roof, and there was another sound, an eerie wailing, like sick cats mewing. She let out a breath.

Tom's nose wrinkled in disgust. 'It's very dirty. Something smells bad.'

Alice went to the table, automatically knocking away the dog which was foraging among the scraps again. She noted the good quality of some of the china, cheek-by-jowl with stained enamel. The mewing behind the curtain increased in volume. She snapped out of her stupor — it was a human cry, not animal.

She pushed aside the sacking and cried out. Crouched side by side on a small bed were two small children, she guessed no more than four and five years old. They wore cotton nightgowns, but grey in colour from poor washing. She'd seen that colour frequently in the East End of London. Soap was an expensive luxury, and energy for rubbing out grime a short commodity after a day's hard work! The children were big-eyed with apprehension.

The taller one said, 'Daisy — had to go — to see to the cow. She said Dad wouldn't be long.'

'We didn't get anything to eat,' the other said.

Alice wasn't surprised. Nothing on the table had looked fit for the dog, let alone children. 'Is there food?' she asked gently.

Frank Crossley came into the room. 'There's food in the storehouse.

Where's Daisy?'

One of the children, a blonde-haired girl, rushed over to him. 'I was scared, Dad — the thunder — '

He patted her head awkwardly. 'Don't be scared. It's gone now.'

'These your children?' Alice was sharp. 'You left them alone here?'

'Daisy was supposed to mind them. What's it to you? You had to be met, didn't you?'

'Where's Jim?' Alice thrust out her chin. She suddenly realised how hungry she was — there'd been nothing to eat since the early breakfast at the hotel. How civilised that appeared in comparison with this.

'He isn't here — and not likely to be. And don't you turn dainty on me, nose in the air. I don't have time to see to the kids — too much to do out there. And Eve — their Ma — she's dead. So don't ask where my missus is.'

Pity for the children, despair for herself and Tom, but above all, anger at Frank Crossley for bringing her here when he knew Jim wasn't there welled up inside of her. 'Where's he gone? Is there no message?'

'Nope. Took off for the goldfields — two months since.'

'But — but — my letter, telling him I was coming?'

Frank Crossley sat on a bench and stooped to take his boots off. He didn't look at her. 'Came just after he'd gone. I opened it — '

'Jim never got it? Never knew? But I wrote to the P & O office, too — in Fremantle. You sent the message to the hotel! Why? Why bring me out here? I'll have to go straight back.'

The man dropped his boots on the earth floor. 'Tonight — in this lot?'

It was Tom who said, 'Can you give us a bed for the night? We'll go in the morning.'

Frank's laugh wasn't pleasant. 'What do you think this is? Hotel?'

The children started to wail again, and he looked at Alice.

'Tell you what I could do.'

'What?' She was suspicious.

He said, with a rush, 'Stop on a while. Since Eve died, I've been in trouble with the kids — and the land. You stay here — as a housekeeper, see to the youngsters. Hang on, hear me out,' he protested at Alice's outraged refusal. 'You don't want to go back to London now, do you? And that young man, Jim, no doubt he'll be back. You can wait here, in return for housework, and helping around the place.'

'So — he is coming back?' Alice cut in swiftly.

He nodded. 'Oh, yes,' he agreed. 'I daresay he will.'

Although Frank looked her straight in the eyes, she didn't believe him, and her bones told her she couldn't trust him. But the children were staring at her now with something like hope in their eyes. She looked around the squalid room. There was a fine, oak dresser in the corner, a floral curtain across the window. Eve? Alice wondered about her. How had she died?

She took off her gloves and hitched her skirt up. 'Show me where the brooms are, then the food. I'll cook for all of us. Give Tom and me a corner to sleep in, then tomorrow we'll see.'

★   ★   ★

A couple of hours later, the floor was swept, the table cleared, and a stew of kangaroo meat and potatoes was simmering in the bake-house — a shed built a few yards from the back door, customary in the pioneer houses. The children's hands and faces had been washed in the abundant rain water outside, and the dog shut out of the house while they ate. Tom had helped, and the children, after an initial shyness, had shown Alice where things were kept.

Frank Crossley said he had to see to the pigs and went out, miraculously reappearing just when the stew was ready.

Tom, practiced with his young

brothers at home, entertained the children, and helped Alice see them to bed. Their bed was in the same area as Frank's, and, as far as Alice could see, there was nowhere else to sleep. She and Tom would have to camp down on the earth floor for the night.

She tucked in the children as best she could. The little girl put her arms up and pulled Alice's head down, whispering, 'Can't you stay? Please! Since Mammy died, it's been horrid. Dad — '

'He doesn't hurt you?'

'No — no. He's so busy all the time. But now, when the others come — since Mammy went — there was fighting, and I'm frightened. You stay, Alice — and Tom.' She let go, putting her thumb in her mouth. Her eyelids started to droop and, as they finally rested against her cheeks, Alice crept from the stuffy room.

She wondered whether, in the morning, the little girl would be able to tell her anything about Jim.

6

Alice woke with a start. She couldn't think why she was lying on the hard ground — only a chink of grey light edged the doorway. She put out her hand. There was a small body next to her! As she touched it, it snuggled closer, and Alice remembered. The little girl must have crept close in the night, as if to make sure Alice didn't escape!

But she'd nowhere to go, Alice thought bitterly, memory flooding back all too clearly. A fine mess she'd made of everything. Tom's even breathing was close, and she touched him reassuringly. For his sake, she must make the best of things, put on a brave face and, above all, she mustn't let Frank Crossley intimidate her. He had no hold over her. She could walk away at any time, but it'd be best to stay a while, find out what she could about

Jim, but she'd only stay on her own terms. Young, female and alone, apart from Tom, in a strange tough country, Alice Foster was, fortunately, still an optimist! She tucked the small body closer to her, and fell asleep again.

A booted foot prodded her side, once, then again, harder. She blinked wide awake, while dawn light lit up the rough-and-ready room.

'Git up. We starts early here. I'm out to see the animals. You just make sure there's breakfast when I come back. Less than an hour.' Frank Crossley, wide-brimmed hat rammed down on his head, loomed over her.

Alice remembered her resolution. Tossing aside the dirty piece of sacking bed cover, she stood up and faced him, drawing herself up tall, adding a dignified inch or two.

'Don't you dare speak like that to me, Mr Crossley. I'm not your servant, nor do I intend to be. You brought us here under false pretences. We don't have to stay but, for the children's sake,

I'll prepare breakfast — not because you very rudely ordered me to.'

A dark scowl darkened Frank Crossley's face, and for a second, Alice thought he might lash out at her, but she stood her ground and out-stared him. The little girl broke the tension.

'Dad, I'll show Alice how to do the damper — and where the creek is.'

The hard eyes softened fractionally, and he looked away, down to the child.

'Right, Elsie, you do that.' But to Alice, he said harshly, 'And get that lazy brother of yours up. I can find him plenty to do outside.'

'He'll get up, but he's not working for you yet. We'll talk about it at breakfast.' She took Elsie's hand. 'And you can show me where to wash.'

Frank picked up a gun from the rack on the wall and went out, not quite sure who'd won that round, but he couldn't help a grudging admiration for young Alice Foster's spirit. A different kettle of fish from Eve, that was certain!

Elsie chattered cheerfully to Alice,

but rarely let go of her hand. They washed in storm water from the previous night, but Elsie said they would have to fetch the day's supply of drinking and cooking water from the creek a mile away. 'Sometimes it dries all up — then there's no water hardly. We can't have it, 'cos the animals must, Dad says. We have damper for breakfast, and billy tea.'

'Damper? Billy tea?'

'Mam showed me, before she died — because I've to look after Dad and Joey, she said — '

'Has Mammy been dead long?' Alice's heart filled with pity for the tear-filled blue eyes.

'Don't know really. About a year, I think. She just got sick.'

'Did the doctor come?'

'Yes. He said she was very ill.' Elsie frowned, trying to get it right even though she didn't understand. 'And that she wasn't the pie near sort of person. What's a pie near, Alice?'

'I think it must be a pioneer.

116

Someone who goes to a new place. Where life and things are hard to do.' She put her arms round the child. 'Tom and me, we're pioneers, in a new country. We need you to show us how to do things out here in Australia. Will you do that, Elsie — you and Joey?'

'I will — if you'll stay.'

'We will — for a while.'

'A while? That's a long time, isn't it?'

'Let's get breakfast.' Alice didn't want to be tied down.

Elsie showed her how to light the wood stove, then mix flour, salt and water, to make damper, a form of instant bread. There was a bowl of new-laid eggs in the store. Alice fried half a dozen, and made tea in a big, enamel billy can. Elsie told her to put it on top of the stove to brew.

'That's how Dad likes it. Mam told me.'

For a child of five, Elsie was amazingly competent. Alice thought sadly that she'd been forced to grow up quickly after her mother's death. Tom came into the bake-house with Joey, and gave a hand carrying the food into the main room. He'd set out plates and mugs, too, and swept the floor. Another child growing up too swiftly. Alice thought he even looked a bit taller this morning, and he wasn't a bit cowed by Frank Crossley's dark, surly look.

They ate in silence. Frank mopped up egg yolk with bits of damper, swilled it down with strong, black tea, and said to Alice, 'Well? Thought on my proposal? You'd make a fine house-keeper from the looks of things. Settled in already.' He was prepared to be conciliatory. In spite of her small size, Alice looked like a worker. The boy, too — might not be such a bad thing either. A bit of meat on him — grow a bit. 'Young 'uns, Elsie and Joey, have took to you. They need a woman here. Get your trunk in here, unpack your things — '

Alice wiped her hands on the none too clean overall she'd found behind the door. 'Mr Crossley, I came here to meet my fiancé, Jim Peterson. I'm prepared to wait here for a while, until he comes back, or I find out where he is.' She glanced at Elsie.

'Told you, he went away — back to the goldfields. Way up past Kalgoorlie. Difficult places to get to — anything could happen up there . . . '

He spoke too swiftly, and Alice's suspicions were strengthened. He knew far more than he was saying. 'Then I know he'll be back for me. I know if he'd received my letter, he'd never have left.'

'That's as maybe. Question is, are you taking up my offer. There's plenty of work for the boy, too. Clearing and fencing's only half done. I've three hundred acres, two cows, horses, pigs, hens — plenty to do. I could use a big, strong lad like him.'

'What'll you pay us then?' Tom piped up.

Frank's whiskers split in two as he opened his mouth and roared with laughter. 'Pay!' he finally spluttered.

'You'll get no pay. Not until the wheat's cropped, and mebbe not then. Depends on the crop. It's not sown yet. All you'll get for now is board and lodging. I'll keep you both in grub.'

'And where's the lodging?' Alice asked.

Frank looked puzzled. 'Behind there.' He jerked his head towards the sacking wall. 'I'll fix up another bed for you. Tom can sleep out here.'

'In the same room as you?'

'Me and the kids. I'll fix up a curtain, partition off a corner. You'll be private, with your own things from the trunk.'

'No thanks, Mr Crossley. You'll have to do better than that, otherwise Tom and I'll be on our way right now.'

She stood up, calculating — with the tiny amount of money she had left, she could, just about, call his bluff. 'Tom, gather our things together — '

'Just a minute, no need to be so hasty. If that don't suit you, you and he can sleep in the shed out back — behind the bake-house. He can shift the stuff that's in there out into the barn, and there's straw — your own quarters.'

'All right then. Just for — a while.' She sat down and, as calmly as she could, poured out more tea for Tom and herself.

★ ★ ★

The 'while' stretched out to four weeks. Alice knew it was four weeks because she and Elsie made a calendar with pictures, showing the months and days. At the end of each day they put a tick; there were twenty-eight ticks across August and September. Every day Alice hoped Jim would arrive, or that there would be some word from him. Nothing! It was as though he'd never existed. Elsie's memory was unclear. She remembered a man with a funny accent who'd worked for Dad for a while, gone away, come back, then gone away again. There was no-one else to ask. Frank Crossley went into town for supplies once a fortnight, and evaded questions about neighbours. Alice wondered about Sarah Winthrop, and where she lived. And Ned McCartney! Practically neighbours he'd said. And what about the mysterious Daisy?

She asked Frank one day, 'Shouldn't Elsie and Joey see other children? Don't you have neighbours?'

'There's folk around — if needs be. Why?' He was suspicious. The last thing he needed was prying neighbours.

'I thought — I'd read — about pioneer communities, getting together. Dances, picnics.' Some sense warned her not to mention either Sarah Winthrop or Ned McCartney.

'We manage,' Frank said shortly. 'You'll not need to bother about dances here.' And that's all he would say about neighbours.

It was hard work, but gradually, as the days passed, Alice sorted out a routine — a curious sort of tranquillity carrying her through the waiting. After her life in the mean back streets of the

East End, the spacious life of fresh air and sunshine beguiled her. Elsie and Joey were no problem, and Frank Crossley was civil enough, but she was always uneasy in his presence, always making sure that the door to their sleeping quarters was barred.

It may have been her imagination, but one night she woke, sure there'd been someone outside — the handle had turned in the darkness, once, twice, then silence. The next night, she put a stout plank across the door as well as the bolt.

Tom took to the life, too, and seemed to have shot up several inches. He was up at dawn, out with Frank, chopping trees, burning down, clearing the virgin land for planting. At first, Frank had tried to order him around. Alice had intervened, but Tom told her he could look after himself. His body hardened, and he lost his city pallor. She hardly recognised him, and was horrified when Frank gave him a rifle and taught him to shoot rabbits and kangaroos. One morning he proudly tossed a couple of rabbits on the table.

Alice screamed. 'Tom? What've you done?'

'Got the supper, Alice. What else?'

'But . . . you should be in school,' she wailed.

Tom shook his head, as though that was an alien concept. 'Where?'

'I don't know. There must be one somewhere. Elsie and Joey, too — '

'Aw, don't worry, Alice. Time enough. I like it fine here.'

Alice was truly desperate. This wasn't what she'd intended at all. They couldn't stay indefinitely. She must find out more about the neighbourhood. There was nothing to stop her walking into Northam, except she didn't know the way. Frank was evasive, and warned her not to go out alone into the bush. If she pressed him to take her into town, he'd always find an excuse, extra jobs for her to do — the children. Alice began to suspect Frank was deliberately keeping her from any outside contact.

To take her mind off her situation, she liked to go out with Tom and help with the land clearing. They both learned to ride, and Alice loved the sense of freedom — she planned to find her own way to Northam on horseback one day.

On one occasion, she came back from the daily trip to the creek for water. She'd got used to hitching up the cart and driving to fill up the barrels. Outside the house was a new cart and a strange horse. Visitors!

Something in Alice's bones warned her to be quiet. It was unusual for Frank to be in the house at this time of the day. She waited a while, lest the noise of her coming had alerted him, then crept near the open window. Cautiously peering in, she saw two men sitting at the table with Frank. They had their backs to her — Frank was facing her. There were whisky bottles on the table, two empty, one still almost full. She bobbed back, pressing her ear to the wooden wall. Frank was speaking loudly. It sounded like an argument.

'So it can't be here. It'll have to be your place.'

'You can't keep this up for ever, Frank. You must be off your head, keeping them here. She'll find out, and then — '

'Not if nobody squawks.' Then in a low mutter which Alice could hardly hear. 'And the kids need someone, since Eve died . . .'

Raucous laughter, tinged with something which made Alice shudder, accompanied the voice of one of the other men. 'I see your game, Frank Crossley. What's she look like then? When are you going to introduce us?'

There was more laughter. When Alice dared to peer in again, Frank was on his feet, pouring more whisky. At that moment he looked up, and for a fraction of a second, she was sure he'd seen her. She didn't wait to find out. She picked up her skirts and ran away from the house as fast as she could.

Later, from the bake-house, where

she and Elsie were making bread, she saw the three men ride off. 'Do you know those men?'

Elsie nodded. 'They come here at night sometimes. Once, Dad sent us to Daisy's, but she didn't come for us until late — and I saw them.'

'What were they doing?'

'I don't know. There was cards — and lots to drink. Dad was cross next day. I'll show you how to make soap now. We haven't any left.' Her mouth was in the determined line Alice had come to recognise. She wasn't going to say anything else.

Alice decided on a plan. She had to get to civilisation. If she could get to Northam, she could ask for Sarah Winthrop, find out if anyone had seen Jim at the Crossley place. Also she must post letters home. She'd written from Fremantle, from the P & O Hotel, and given Frank letters for him to post, but she felt sure he'd never sent them. There was no word from home, and she longed for news. She hadn't told the

127

family the situation, simply that she and Tom loved the sunshine, and Australia; that Jim was delayed, but expected any day.

Tom agreed to help find the way to Northam. There was a crude signpost pointing to the town, but the track petered out in the bush. Alice wanted to chart the different paths farther and farther until they hit the main dirt road into the town. It became imperative to her as the days passed. Soon it would be summer, much hotter, with the inevitable fear or drought. To venture too far into the bush without knowing the way would be even more risky then.

Frank Crossley's behaviour was becoming more and more worrying. When he'd ridden off with the two men, he'd stayed away all night, and had been in a bad mood for days, short tempered and morose. She didn't like the way he kept looking at her, but she liked it even less when he started to be pleasant, following her around, asking if he could help carry the water barrels, smiling at her, dropping hints about how lonely it was being a widower.

One afternoon, she and Tom were out riding, following a promising-looking wide track, when a horse-rider appeared in the distance.

'Tom — look — that rider must be coming from somewhere. We must be on the right track.'

'We can ask him anyway.'

'Thank goodness.' Alice spurred on her horse, reined back, her heart beating rapidly — the figure was familiar. It took off its hat in a sweeping gesture, and she saw it was, indeed, Ned McCartney.

He cantered up to them, a broad smile on his face. Alice remembered how attractive he was. After being cooped up with Frank Crossley for weeks, he looked even more wonderfully strong, handsome and wholesome!

'Why, it's Alice Foster and Tom. Alice, you're prettier than ever. Australia suits you, I see. Tom — almost a man now. Is it the climate, d'you think?'

He dismounted, and went to help Alice do the same, holding out his arms to catch her. How she longed to fling herself in them and stay there! He held her for a second, looking deep into her eyes, then set her on her feet, took the reins, and tethered both their horses, along with Tom's.

'Now tell me how you are? I've meant to ride over and enquire of Crossley how you fared, but my mother's been ill and I've been occupied with family matters. What luck to run into you here. And where is your young man? Are you married? I take it an unkindness not to have been invited to the wedding.'

'I'm not married,' Alice had to say reluctantly, 'but soon will be. Jim — '

'He's gone away,' Tom broke in, 'and I don't think he'll — '

'Tom! Mr McCartney doesn't want to hear all this. Hush now. Things are perfectly fine. Jim has been delayed — at the goldfields. It won't be long before he's back. I'm sorry to hear about your mother. I hope she's recovered.'

'Not quite yet.' Ned frowned — the abrupt change of subject was so transparent. 'So, where are you staying until Jim returns?'

Tom burst in, 'We're having to work for Frank Crossley, and it — '

'Tom, that'll do! Mr Crossley is letting us stay with him — to look after his children — temporarily.'

'But you can't stay there. Unchaperoned — alone!'

'Tom is my chaperone,' Alice said haughtily, hating the pity in Ned's eyes. 'We are perfectly all right. Come, Tom, we must be getting back. Nice to meet you again, Mr McCar — '

'It was Ned on board ship,' he chided, unease clutching his heart as he looked at Alice's stiff figure and Tom's troubled eyes. 'I can be of help, Alice, if you're in trouble. A few miles up this track, there's a fork — the left hand track takes you to our farm, five miles farther on. It's signposted

— Koolingup Farm.'

'Thank you, but I'm sure we shan't be needing those directions. I expect you're very busy with your family and friends.' She mounted her horse quickly, knowing if she stayed another second she'd blurt out all her troubles; her fear of Frank Crossley, and her concern about Jim's whereabouts.

Ned watched her as she wheeled her mount around.

'Goodbye — Ned,' she called, desperately keeping her voice calm to stop the quaver. It came out ice-cool, and he turned to his own horse.

Tom looked from one to the other, torn by indecision. They needed help. Why shouldn't they ask for it? 'Ned . . . ' he started to say.

'Tom!' his sister shouted.

'Oh, drat it.' With a despairing look at Ned, Tom followed Alice, and it wasn't until he'd caught her up that he realised they hadn't even asked the way to Northam.

As if to emphasise their folly in

cutting off Ned's offer of help, Frank Crossley was in a foul mood on their return. He was waiting by the fenced-in paddock. Alice realised, with a sinking feeling, that he'd been drinking.

'Where you been?' he shouted. 'You've no business riding them horses off the farm. They're for work, not fun.'

'If you won't tell me how to get to Northam, we'll have to find our own way.' Alice was defiant.

'What's in Northam for you?'

'News of Jim. You can't keep us here. We need to meet other people.'

'What for? Jim Peterson'll never be back here. Settle yourself for that.'

'If I thought that for a second, I'd be off this place now,' Alice retorted, all her suspicions aroused again. 'What haven't you been telling me, Frank Crossley?'

'Nothing to tell you. How're you going to leave here — you've no money?'

'You should pay us.' Tom came to stand by Alice. He was almost as tall as

133

she was now. 'Pay both of us — we've worked hard here.'

'Pay you? I feed you, don't I?'

'I'll get a job. Hire myself out!'

'Who'd have you?' Frank sneered.

'Ned McCartney. Why didn't you ask him, Alice?' Tom blurted out.

Frank looked as though someone had struck him, his bravado oozing away.

'How do you know McCartney?'

'We met him on the boat.' Alice shot a warning glance at Tom.

'I don't want you having anything to do with that lot,' Frank growled — but he was worried.

'It's nothing to do with you,' Alice said, far more calmly than she felt. She'd been a fool to turn down Ned's offer. For Tom's sake, she should swallow her foolish pride and appeal to Ned to get them away. Yet, could she just walk away from Elsie and Joey? That would be hard.

'Aw — I wish I'd never set eyes on the pair of you.' Frank turned on his heel. Things had gone from bad to worse since Eve's death. He sought out the only true solace he knew — the whisky bottle!

That evening, Alice made up her mind. She would ask Ned for help. Just how, she couldn't figure, especially if Frank forbade them to ride off the farm. She settled the children, and to avoid Frank, went early to their sleeping quarters in the shed. It was rough-hewn, but she'd made it cosy enough, and it was shaded by a clump of eucalyptus trees.

Tom was busy skinning rabbits and possums. He was thinking if he could get into town, he could sell the skins, and they'd have money to get away. He, too, had decided to go independently to Ned, and ask for help. Young as he was, he divined they were in danger, especially Alice. He'd shot a score of rabbits, and trapped the same number of possums. He'd hide them from Frank and store them in a sack until he could get into town . . .

Alice lay on her straw mattress and wrote her diary. Someday, when she and Jim were old, they'd get it out and read about these tiresome days. She wrote she'd met Ned again. She thought about him, conjured up his dark-blue eyes, his hands on the reins . . . the diary slid to the ground, she closed her eyes, and fell asleep.

She couldn't breathe. She twisted, turned — there was something on the bed, an animal — heavy — suffocating her — pressing her down. The smell, stale drink — a sharp, prickly whiskery face on hers! She fought and pushed, but the more she struggled, the more it pinned her down.

The voice was slurred. 'Now, Miss Alice, don't you fight. It's time you and I came to an understanding — a lesson — time to wed — '

Alice, terrified, then furious, screamed as loudly as she could, before the hand clamped her lips. The heavy body pressed her down and down. She was weakening —

The door burst open, and Tom, wild, fists flailing, flung himself on to Frank, and pulled at him. 'Get away from her,' he yelled. 'Alice!'

Frank, surprised, turned, relaxed his grip.

Alice bit him hard.

He yelped, released her, turned to fend off Tom.

Tom was on him, hands round his throat, shaking him.

But Frank was stronger. He plucked away Tom's fingers, picked him up and hurled him across the room.

Alice's scream was the last thing Tom heard as he struck his head on the corner of their iron travelling trunk which had held their clothes.

'Tom!' Alice rushed across to him, took his head, felt the warm stickiness of blood, saw he was deadly pale. 'You — you've killed him!'

'Ssh — you'll wake the kids — ' Frank swayed, glaze-eyed. 'He shouldn't've come at me like that.' He took a step towards them.

Alice recoiled, and spat out like a tigress. 'Don't you dare come near. If he's dead . . . '

'He's not dead. I see 'im breathe.'

The blood oozed a little, spreading stain on the earth floor. It was just as before — his leg — on the boat. The boat — Ned! Ned had saved him then. He could do it again.

Alice hissed out, 'Get the cart. Hitch up the horses — both of them. Get sheets — blankets — '

'Who're you giving orders — ' Frank was finding it difficult to stand.

Alice picked up a pail of water and flung it over him.

'Just do it, Frank. Unless you want to be charged with murder!'

He blinked, spluttered, shook his head, but went out of the door.

Alice tore strips off a linen shirt, and made a pad to staunch the blood. If only she could get to Ned on time — he'd save Tom! She heard the rattle of cart wheels outside. Now, if he wanted to, Frank Crossley could pass out — and, she hoped, it would be for ever. Fear gave her superhuman strength as she picked up Tom's limp body . . .

7

Frank Crossley made a half-hearted attempt to help carry Tom out to the cart, but he was so far gone in drink, Alice was terrified he'd drop the boy. It was a relief, at least, to see he'd heaped sacks and blankets on the bottom of the cart.

'Where are you taking him? Best stay here. He'll be all right in the morning. Only a little knock. You can't drive this — '

'Can't I?' Alice's face was grim. 'Watch me. And you — you get back in the house — to the children.'

'That's your job.' He stood by the horse's head, holding on to the reins. 'Mine's to drive.'

'Oh, get away.' Alice snatched the reins from him, leaned down and pushed him hard. He staggered back, and the last she saw of him, he was sprawled in an untidy heap in the doorway. She prayed Elsie and Joey wouldn't wake, but her family came first.

Fortune, for once, was with her. As darkness fell, a full moon rose over the bush, picking out the track she and Tom had taken only hours earlier. He lay inert, his pallor made more deathly by the rising moon. The track was narrow, rutted and bumpy. Earlier, the horses had picked their way delicately, but now the cart simply rolled on.

The track looked different by night. Scrub pressed thickly on either side. There were rustlings, yelps, and once, the bounding shape of a large kangaroo, eerie and threatening by night. Was this the spot where they'd met Ned? A mile along, then a fork, he'd said. How big a fork? There were so many places where tracks branched away from the main one. Once or twice she panicked, certain she'd missed the turning and was blundering into the bush, where surely, they'd both die. She fought off the terrors. She'd put Tom in this situation, and she'd get him out. She tried to relax, concentrate, ignore the faint, dreadful, snoring breaths which were coming from the back of the cart.

At last, she reached a fork — a pronounced one — and she leaned forward. She saw a wooden sign pointing like an angelic finger straight down quite a good dirt road. *Koolingup Farm.* With a prayer of thanks, she sent the cart bowling more confidently along. The eucalyptus trees were taller here, arching over the road, blocking out the light, but the horses tossed their heads, and by instinct, she gave them full rein, not knowing that was doing the right thing.

Glancing fearfully over her shoulder, she saw Tom had tossed away his coverings, was moving restlessly, his head turning from side to side.

'Oh, Tom. Be still — please. We must be nearly there.'

She reckoned it was an hour since the fork. Five miles had Ned said? Ten? A few, that was it. How many was a few? She wished she'd taken more notice, but she'd been so busy putting on a brave front, not letting Ned see how pleased she'd been to see him . . .

The road surface changed again. It was smoother, wider, fences either side, a long, long driveway. Round a corner and a blaze of lights from a long, low house, wide verandas running its length, carriages drawn up outside. She could hear music — party? She prayed Ned was home.

She drew in the horses by wide-open double doors. She had an impression of light and colour, of startled faces gathering in the entrance, as she leaped out and ran towards the lights, oblivious of the fact that she was in her nightgown, one of Tom's jackets around her shoulders, hair streaming loose.

A stern-faced man ran down the stairs.

'Get out, miss. What are you doing here? Can't you see . . . '

The man was roughly thrust aside

and there, finally, was Ned.

'Alice! You're hurt. There's blood on you.'

'No — no. It's Tom. He's outside in the cart. It's his blood. Ned, I'm so frightened. He may be dying.'

'We'll see. Aunt Edie, can you look after Alice?'

A tall, handsome woman, whose face was vaguely familiar came over and took Alice by the arm. 'Of course I can. You look as though a hot bath and a hot drink would cheer you up.'

'No — please. Let me be with Tom. The journey — it was so bumpy — I'm scared — his head — '

Ned had already run out to the cart, and the two men were carrying Tom through the hall, carefully supporting his head. His shirt was soaked bright red, and darker, crusted blood matted his hair.

'Tom — ' Alice cried, but Ned was by her side, reassuring her.

'You did well to bring him. Tell me what happened later. Go with Edie

144

now, and I'll come as soon as I know what's wrong.'

'We're spoiling your party.' Suddenly, now the strain of getting to Ned had gone, Alice remembered her manners.

He smiled. 'Nearly over. It's for Tilly. I think you saw her in London. It's an engagement party. A small one, because of Mother. Now, I must go to Tom.'

A warm smile, and he was gone, leaving Alice with a squeezed out sort of feeling. So Tilly had finally made it. What a lucky girl — to have Ned McCartney, and, Alice looked round wistfully, all this fine house, too. Still, if Tom was all right, that's all she could ask for herself. She was just lucky to have got him to Ned!

Aunt Edie had filled a bath tub with hot water, and the luxury of a long soak restored Alice's spirits. Ned's aunt fussed around her, bringing clothes and a shawl, reassuringly matter-of-fact, treating as an everyday occurrence the appearance of a wild, blood-spattered girl, flying up the front steps.

'Ned is so good,' she told Alice proudly. 'Everyone, for miles around, comes to him. He's working hard to establish a hospital for the region, but it's going to cost a fortune.'

A dreadful thought struck Alice. How was she going to pay for Tom's treatment? She owed Ned for the leg injury on the boat, although he'd said she'd repaid the debt by helping him with nursing.

'I'll leave you to rest a while, dear. I must attend to our guests. I'll tell Ned where you are.'

The room in which Edie had left Alice was cool and restful. From the swish of wheels outside, voices raised in farewell, she guessed it must be at the front of the house. It was another world from Frank Crossley's farm. She shuddered at the memory of his whisky breath and heavy body on hers. How could she possibly go back — after this glimpse of a civilised way of life? But she had to.

She and Tom were too much in debt

already to Ned McCartney, and she couldn't burden him further with her troubles, especially since he had Tilly here with him now. And Frank Crossley held the key to Jim's fate, she was sure of that. She owed it to Jim to stay. She closed her eyes, made herself relax in the peaceful room, and tried to think what to do next.

A soft footfall behind her, a touch on her hair, and Ned was there.

'Tom — ' She started up, her tone questioning.

He gently pushed her back. 'He will be all right, thanks to you. I've sewn the wound, but he's lost a lot of blood, and I'll have to keep an eye on him for a few days.' He smiled ruefully. 'Poor Tom, he's a bit accident prone.'

'It's my fault he gets into these situations. I'm beginning to think I'm bad luck for him.'

'Nonsense. He's a tough lad. Now, tell me how it happened tonight.'

'He fell — an accident,' Alice said hastily. 'He hasn't said anything to you?'

'No — he's still unconscious, but should come round soon.'

'I — we — must go. We've imposed on you long enough. Your engagement party . . . '

'That's not your worry — and you most certainly aren't going back. Tom mustn't be moved.'

'But I — we can't pay you.'

He frowned. 'I've not asked for payment.'

'No — but — we can't, not again. When Jim comes — he'll have money. All I have is . . . ' She fished for the cord around her neck — the emergency fund her father had given her the night before she sailed away. Well, this was an emergency. 'This ring — it's gold. It's my mother's wedding ring. Please take it, until I can pay you.'

'Alice! I don't want your mother's ring.'

'Please — please! You don't know — I'm so grateful.'

Ned saw her distress and agitation, and took both her hands in his, the ring held fast between them. Alice was sure he must hear the beating of her heart. His eyes held hers — she saw, and felt, their passionate depths, and tried to withdraw her hands, but he slowly raised them to his lips, saying softly, 'I will keep your ring — for the time being. You are a brave girl, Alice, and we are friends.' He bent his head and kissed her prisoned fingers. 'And now, we'll see how Tom's getting along.'

'I must go back then.'

'Impossible tonight.'

'But — I took the cart, and there's the children. I can drive safely, and now I know the way — '

'The Crossley children? They're in your charge?'

'Yes. They'll be frightened if I'm not there.'

'I dislike the whole idea of you being there. Frank Crossley has some evil associates — the place has a bad reputation. I'm surprised at your fiancé leaving you there.'

'It wasn't his intention. He didn't know — he didn't get my letter.'

Alice was indignant. Gratitude to Ned, and her own pride, stopped her saying more, but there was an unease between them, as he led her to the room where Tom lay, head bandaged, eyes closed.

Ned took his wrist, laid his hand on the boy's forehead.

'His pulse is steady, and there's no fever — all thanks to you for bringing him here so promptly. If you're determined to go back to Crossley's, I'll bring Tom over when he's better.'

'I'll fetch him. You mustn't trouble.'

'You, Miss Alice, will obey the doctor, or I won't answer for the consequences.'

She bowed her head. 'May I sit with him tonight then?'

'If you wish. The couch over there is comfortable. Aunt Edie will bring some cushions. I shall look in from time to time — my room is next door to this. Call me if you have any cause for alarm.'

Alice stayed by Tom all night, watching, with relief, a little colour creep back into his cheeks. Once he opened his eyes, smiled and reached for her hand. His lips moved. 'Tell Ned.'

She shook her head fiercely, and said firmly, 'No. Don't tell him anything. It was an accident. You fell.'

Tom sighed wearily, closed his eyes and dropped her hand.

Just as dawn broke, Alice slipped out of the house. Tom was sleeping peacefully, his breathing normal. He'd be quite safe. It took her a while to find the cart and horses, which had been stabled round the back of the house. In the daylight, the house looked even larger; there were many outbuildings, and rolling farmland fell away on all sides. It all looked very prosperous. Alice drove quietly down the drive, sadness in her heart to leave the McCartney house behind.

Her heart sank even further as she approached the Crossley land. In contrast, it was unkempt, neglected, much of it still scrub covered. The sun was well up when she drove to the door. Elsie and Joey came running to meet her, pulling her hands and arms, grasping her legs.

'We thought you'd gone away for ever.' Elsie cried. 'You weren't in the shed this morning. Nor Tom. Where is he?'

'He's just gone away for a while. He'll be back soon. Where's your father?'

'He's inside. He slept on and on. We thought he'd never wake up.'

Pity he did, Alice thought acidly, but she had to tackle him. 'Be good children and feed the hens now. I'll be along in a minute to cook us up some breakfast.'

They ran off happily. All was well in their world — Alice was back!

Frank Crossley sat at the table, pale and subdued, an enamel coffee pot in his hand. 'You came back then. Cart and horses safe, I hope.'

'They are.'

He gulped down the hot liquid. 'And — the boy?' he muttered.

Alice took a clean china cup from the dresser, sat down opposite him, and slowly poured herself some coffee. She sensed his fear; she'd use it as a weapon. Coolly, she sipped her drink, taking her time, until Frank could bear it no longer.

'Well? Tom? He's all right, isn't he?'

'He is — no thanks to you.' He sat back in relief, but Alice swiftly added, 'You assaulted me, and nearly killed Tom. I should tell the police.'

Frank laughed. 'Who'd believe you? Fell and hit his head, that's all.'

'I'll tell them, shall I? And Dr McCartney — he'll back me up.'

'Did you tell him?'

'No, I didn't. Tom's still there. But if you lay a finger on Tom, or on me, I shall certainly tell him what happened.'

'I'd taken a drink,' he mumbled. 'Don't recall touching you.'

'I recall it very well — every detail.

Just you remember that.'

Frank Crossley slunk out of the room, fuming. For the moment, he was beaten, but he'd get his own back in time.

* * *

The next few days were routine — and hard labour for Alice. Frank behaved himself, didn't drink, and was civil. She worked on the land to make up for Tom's absence — back-breaking work; chopping trees, digging roots. Her hands were calloused and dirt-grimed, but she didn't mind. When Tom was back, they'd leave, but not until she'd had a show-down with Frank about Jim.

At the end of the week, Ned sent a message saying he'd be bringing Tom back next day. Alice cleaned the house, washed her hair, and waited. The carriage came at mid-day, and to Alice's amazement, Frank Crossley, spruced up in a new jacket, hair and whiskers combed, came out to meet it stepping forward to shake, first, Tom's, and then Ned McCartney's hand.

'I see you're fit again. Tom. Nasty accident he had, doctor. Would've brought him over myself, but Alice here insisted — and, of course, one of us had to stay with the kiddies.'

Tom and Alice both gaped. Ned looked mystified, even more so when Frank invited them into the house for tea.

'Alice's been baking, I'll be bound. There's sure to be a cake or two. Before your return trip, doctor.'

Ned looked at Alice and Tom. What was Crossley up to? He'd only met the man once, in Fremantle, years ago, when he was a medical student. He'd attended to wounds from a pub brawl. Frank had been drunk, abusive and violent. A miracle conversion? It didn't accord with local gossip. Tom had told him nothing of their circumstances, but Ned didn't have to be a mind reader to realise that the boy was desperate to confide in him — only loyalty to his sister preventing it. Alice avoided his eyes altogether.

'Thank you, no. I've patients to visit farther down the road. I'll see you again in a week or so, Tom. If you'll permit him to ride over, Mr Crossley?'

'Of course, of course. Anything in Tom's interests. Alice, the children are waiting for you indoors. They'll be shy of the doctor here. And, while you're here, Doctor McCartney, I'd like your advice on a horse of mine. It's over in the paddock.'

'But I'm not a vet.' Ned was anxious to talk to Alice, but Frank had him by the arm.

'No, but you're a judge of horseflesh. If you'd be good enough . . . '

'Alice, I'll see you in a moment,' Ned called to her.

She looked at him directly for the first time, eyes appealing, then turned away and went with Tom into the house.

Ned stood with Frank by the

paddock rail. There were two horses in the field.

'They both look healthy.'

'Piebald's got a limp. Nothing much. What I really wanted was to thank you for looking after young Tom. It would embarrass Alice if she heard. And if there's anything to pay . . . '

'Pay?' Ned tipped his head back in astonishment. Frank Crossley had little spare money, it was common knowledge in the neighbourhood — his land was poor, and he had little skill with it. Rumours were, he augmented his income in other, probably nefarious, ways. He was notoriously tight-fisted. To offer to pay for Tom's medical treatment was totally out of character. Ned said slowly, 'Payment's been taken care of. I shouldn't have thought it was your concern.'

'That's where you're wrong. Tom's my concern. You see, Doctor McCartney, Alice and I are to be wed.'

It was rare for Ned to be rendered speechless, but this was one such occasion. His mind grappled with the idea of Alice and Frank Crossley, rejected it, then was filled with grinding fury. 'You and Alice — to be married!'

'Right.' Frank smirked hideously. 'Her idea, too. I would never have asked, but she loves the kids so — '

'But — she has a fiancé, Jim Peterson. She came out to marry him.'

'Aw, he'll not be back. It's none of my business, but I reckon he changed his mind. I shouldn't say, but she's well out of that. Peterson's a bad character, not an ideal husband for a pretty young girl like Alice.' He came closer to Ned, with a backward glance towards the house. 'Truth to tell, I don't think she much minds. She says she came out here to marry, and marry she's determined to do. So, I don't mind obliging!'

Ned stepped away, rage and anger blinding his eyes and his judgement. Visions of Frank Crossley, beaten to pulp at his feet, swam in his brain. He drew back his fists, his eyes flashing wild torment. He knew he'd kill Crossley if he stayed. Turning on his heel, he strode to the carriage.

Seconds later, Alice at the doorway of the house, saw it driven at breakneck pace along the track. He hadn't come to say goodbye as he'd promised her. Tears blinded her eyes, so she didn't see Frank rubbing his hands in delight.

'That,' he chortled, 'will settle her hash, and he won't be coming round here again.' Anyway, it was partly true. He wouldn't mind marrying Alice. Once she was legally shackled, he'd soon show her who was boss! Delighted with himself, he went into the paddock and saddled up his horse. Time to reassert his authority — he'd been without a bit of fun for too long. He rode off towards Northam, taking the opposite track from Ned, still chuckling at his cleverness.

8

In the days following Ned's visit, Alice's natural resilience deserted her. She saw his abrupt departure as relief that he was rid of the responsibility of Tom and, to a lesser extent, herself. That she should believe him capable of such behaviour was proof of her low state of mind. She despaired of ever leaving Crossley's. She realised that she'd counted on Ned's assistance, but now he'd abandoned her, there was no hope.

To make matters worse, Frank Crossley's manner had changed. He'd returned from Northam with a bolder, even more aggressive manner than before. He drove Tom hard, in spite of Alice's protests that her brother needed to take things easier for a while.

'If he don't like it, he can clear off. In fact, perhaps that'd be best — one less mouth to feed!'

Alice drew herself up and said, more bravely than she felt, 'If Tom goes — I go!'

'Oh, no. You stay, miss. You'd best think of settling for good. I've a mind to marry you. Make you a respectable woman. Can't have folk gossiping.'

Alice recoiled in disgust. Marry Frank Crossley! She'd sooner die in the bush, with a pile of snakes for company. As for people gossiping! 'Who is there to know in this place? No-one ever comes here. You're keeping us prisoners.'

'That I'm not. You can walk away at any time. Didn't you go off to the McCartney's — stealing my horses.'

Alice turned away. It was useless. There was no way out. Even Tom was turning against her. He begged her to send him to Ned for help. Ned had been so good to him when he was recovering at the farm — it was only Alice's stubborn pride that prevented them leaving. He could work for Ned to get some money, then find a place of their own.

'Oh, Tom, it's hopeless. We'd never have the money.'

'Write to Father then. Maybe times are better there. I can take a letter to post. Ned's told me the way to Northam. I can walk. We can't moulder away here, Alice. Jim Peterson'll never come now.'

Each fed the other's despair, but Alice still clung to the hope that Jim would turn up one day. Without that, life was meaningless — except for Elsie and Joey. At least they gave her a purpose in life. She tried to avoid Frank as much as possible, and was always careful to keep their sleeping quarters well barricaded.

One evening, at supper, Frank announced he was having a party. Alice couldn't believe her ears. Her hopes rose, but Frank dashed them straight away.

'No need to look like that. It isn't a party any of you are coming to. It's been too quiet around here for too long.'

'Dad — is it those men?' Elsie's eyes were big and fearful, and Frank had the grace to look flustered.

He put his hand on his daughter's head, ruffling her curls.

'Now, don't you be worrying. I'll see they don't come quarrelling round you. Fact is, you won't see them at all. You and Joey can go and sleep with Alice and Tom. It's just a card game — a few of the farmers around here.'

'And their wives?' Alice asked without hope.

'It isn't that sort of party. You just cook up some good grub for tomorrow, then you can disappear — and don't put your noses outside once folk arrive, or there'll be trouble.'

All the next day, Alice felt a growing sense of foreboding. She tried to ignore it — blamed it on the weather, which daily grew hotter, with a fierce heat like nothing she'd known before. The bake-house was stifling and, as she cooked bread and pies, sweat poured from her.

The children were unusually fretful, too, and it wasn't merely the heat, which never seemed to bother them. Alice presumed they were accustomed to it. It had to be the idea of the party which unsettled them. It sounded harmless enough, though Alice feared there'd be a deal of drinking. Yet she'd seen plenty of that at home in the East End pubs, and that hadn't frightened her like this.

'We'll have our own party, in our shed.' She tried to cheer them up. 'I'll make a cake, just for us, and your dad brought some oranges from Northam. I'll make some juice.'

'Mammy never liked the parties,' Elsie volunteered.

'Why not?' Alice took off her overall, and pulled back her hair. The baking was done so they could go outside — it'd be cooler by the creek.

'They were noisy, and we couldn't sleep.'

'We'll be all right. We're all going to sleep together. We'll be away from the party. Let's go and fetch the water. Maybe we can bathe — we're done here.'

In the cooler evening air, they splashed about and played in the creek, Alice noting with alarm how low the water level was now that summer drew on. Frank had warned it frequently dried up for days on end, and then they had a real problem. Alice prayed they wouldn't be at Crossley's that long! Tom joined them. Frank had grudgingly told the boy he could stop work early, while he got ready for his party.

As they came back from the creek, Alice saw strange horses tethered by the paddock; a couple of riders were dismounting — one touched his hat to her, while the other stared curiously at her in such a way that she felt uneasy. They reminded her of the two men in the train. She'd be glad to be safely holed up in their shed.

Tom carried out a basket of food to

the orchard, away from the house. Alice tried to make it into a happy picnic party, but the children were subdued and kept glancing in the direction of the house.

It was Elsie who finally said, 'I'd like to go to bed now, please, Alice,' and that was the end of the picnic!

At first, it was quiet, but as night fell, noise began to carry from the house. It grew louder, and at one point, they heard carriage wheels. After that, female voices mingled with those of the men; fiddle music began to play, stamping and cheering, and always the clash of glasses.

Elsie and Joey fell asleep quite quickly, but as the noise increased, they woke up and began to cry. Alice lit a candle, but was ever fearful of fire. Everything was tinder-dry and their straw mattresses could catch light in an instant from a stray spark. The night was still, the coverings on the doors and windows in the house flung aside in the heat. Noise streamed out. Elsie clung on to Alice.

'Hush — it's only a bit of singing and dancing,' she tried to reassure, but Elsie wailed more loudly.

'They'll be fighting. Dad'll be hurt.'

'Shall I go and see? Tell them to be quieter,' Tom offered.

'No!' Alice was growing angry. It was well after midnight, and the party seemed to be getting wilder by the minute. 'I'll go. There are ladies there. I'll talk to them. You look after the children, and watch out for that candle.'

Her inclination was to rush over and demand a little more quiet decorum, but instinctive caution prevailed. As she neared the house, she could see through the front entrance. The sacking doorway had been torn down; men and women were sitting drinking, one or two dancing to the fiddle music. Alice was not naîve enough to imagine the women were respectable, married ladies — they were too provocatively and scantily clad. It was doubtful she could appeal to them!

She crept nearer and saw, through the window, the room behind the sacking curtain. A card game was in progress. Frank presided over a pile of money, and there was little noise from that part of the house. It looked like serious business. To Alice's horror, she saw a hand gun placed casually on a chair next to him. As she watched, he pulled money towards him and dropped it into a leather bag. Two of the men pushed back their chairs angrily and, moments later, Alice saw them come out of the house.

She shrank back — it seemed they must see her, but they sat down on a wooden bench some yards way, pulling out pipes and a bottle. All idea of confronting the party-goers vanished. She thought she'd be lucky to get safely back to the shed. Certainly, none of the men looked at all amenable to reason in their present moods. The voices of the two men carried clearly to her.

'Frank's a lucky devil tonight. He's skint me.'

'Generous with his liquor though.'

'Serves his purpose. Fuddles some, and that makes them easy meat for Crossley.'

'Where's that girl he's got tucked away then? Shall us go looking?'

Alice froze in terror.

The men drew on their pipes. 'Naw — best not to cross Frank. Look what happened to Jim Peterson!'

'Ah — that was different. Not likely for either of us to land up in Fremantle Prison. We know too much about Crossley's crooked games!'

'Peterson'll rot there for ever, so it seems.'

'He will, if Frank's got any influence there.'

'Which, I believe, he has!'

Both men burst into raucous laughter, slapped each other's shoulders, and then, to Alice's intense relief, went back inside.

She stayed where she was for some minutes, not daring to move in case she attracted attention. Had she heard aright? Jim — in prison! She had heard it. Rot for ever — the words seared her brain. With that knowledge, she pushed away all pride and thoughts of Tom's and her plight.

Silently, she went back to the shed, and told her brother what he must do.

'Thank goodness. It's dreadful about Jim, but at least it's brought you to your senses,' he cried gratefully.

'Just be careful no-one sees you leaving. Lead the horse well way before you ride him, and be careful when you come back. Keep clear of the house.' She gave him a hug. 'Good luck, Tom.'

She watched him go towards the paddock, then bolted the door and settled down to wait.

Gradually, the noise subsided, and the children slept. Alice heard the carriage leave on an upsurge of cheering, then, one by one, the riders left. She hoped Frank would be too befuddled to notice one of his horses had gone. It was towards dawn, when all was silent, that Tom came creeping back.

'All arranged,' he yawned, to Alice's anxious query. 'Beyond the creek, at mid-day tomorrow. He'll wait for you.'

'What did . . . ?'

But Tom, worn out by his two-way ride, fell fast asleep.

Alice let him sleep on in the morning, whilst she and the children went apprehensively into the house. It was chaotic; dirty crockery and glasses, bottles strewn everywhere. The fiddler was slumped in a corner, snoring loudly. Frank was stretched out on his bed, dead to the world, and likely to remain so for several hours. Alice tidied up round them, and sent the children to feed the animals. Later, she woke Tom so he could keep an eye on Elsie and Joey, then went to saddle one of the horses.

Ned was sitting on an upturned log by the creek, waiting for her. 'Alice!'

He helped her dismount, and they sat side-by-side on the log. She couldn't

171

help herself; she leaned against him, and he put his arm around her.

'I'm glad it's not true, Alice.'

'What?' In a moment, she'd talk to him about Jim. For now, she just enjoyed his presence, the feel of him close.

'You're not marrying Frank Crossley. Tom told me it was a pack of lies.'

'Marry! Him! Whatever . . . ?'

'Hush. Crossley told me.' He pulled her back beside him.

'And you believed him? Ned! How could you possibly imagine I could ever . . . Is that why you rushed away — why you never came back?'

She looked at him so reproachfully, he took her hands and bent his head towards her. He kissed her, a kiss meant to be one of reaffirming friendship, but as soon as their lips touched, it was a kiss of passion — a lover's kiss!

Alice could not resist. She drank its sweetness like one deprived of sustenance, then pulled away in guilt. 'Tilly! I'm sorry.'

'Tilly?'

'You're engaged.'

Puzzlement, then laughter. 'Alice, what a pair we are for misunderstandings. Tilly's engaged to my younger brother — not to me. She came out on the next boat after ours, she was so unhappy to be parted from him. But that's not why you sent Tom so dramatically last night — to speak of Tilly.'

Alice was ashamed. She'd forgotten about Jim in the joy of seeing Ned, and knowing he wasn't engaged to Tilly. But she was engaged to Jim, wasn't she? And Jim was in trouble. She told Ned what she'd heard the previous night.

'So I do need your help. I'm powerless on my own. What can I do?'

Ned, too, had momentarily forgotten Jim Peterson. He thought awhile before he spoke. 'We must find out firstly if it's true, then why he is in prison. Fortunately I know the prison governor, and my uncle is a lawyer in Perth, so it shouldn't be too difficult.'

'I must go to Jim, but if Frank finds out . . . '

'You mustn't tell him.' Ned looked worried. 'I'd take you to Fremantle myself, but Mother is still very ill. I need to stay here for a while longer, but you must go at once, and take Tom, of course. I'll telegraph the prison today and make arrangements for you to go to Fremantle if we find Jim's really there. Tomorrow morning, early, I'll bring the carriage to the road past Crossley's to take you and Tom to Northam station. Pack a bag — you may have to stay in Fremantle for a few days.'

She knew there was no alternative. 'I will repay you, one day — I know it.'

'It doesn't matter,' Ned said simply. 'Go back now, tell Frank you're going for supplies. He can't prevent you, and if you're not at the end of the track by eight o'clock tomorrow I shall come to the farm and fetch you myself.'

'I hate to leave the children.'

'It can't be helped. They were on

their own with him before you came. And however wicked he is, he won't harm them.' His hands lingered on her waist as he helped her mount. 'Take care, Alice, and never fear, we'll get to the bottom of the mystery.'

But as he watched her ride away, his heart was heavy with misgiving. Ever since Frank's revelation that he was going to marry Alice, Ned had been distracted and uneasy. Also, he'd been making his own enquiries in the district about Jim Peterson, and the rumours he'd heard hadn't been reassuring for Alice's future.

9

When Alice returned, she primed Tom. They must act as normal or Frank would suspect something and prevent them leaving. So, next day, they were all up at dawn going about the day's routine, feeding the stock, working the land. Tom went fencing with Frank, but planned to slip back on some pretext. Then he and Alice would hurry on foot down the track to meet Ned.

She'd packed a small bag, and settled Elsie and Joey to play in the orchard. She felt dreadful about leaving them, but had to harden her heart.

All went according to plan, and they'd skirted the paddock and would have been round the bend near the track to the road in minutes, when Frank Crossley came riding towards them. He spurred on his horse, blocking their path.

It was half past seven — Ned may already be waiting for them. Alice was in an agony of indecision. Could she outrun Frank? On his big horse, he was menacing, a more threatening figure than usual. The hunting gun he carried everywhere was slung around his shoulder. It was no use trying to run away, he'd catch them in seconds. Her only chance was to brazen it out. They were free agents and could go where they pleased — but she was frightened — for Tom, and Ned, too, if he came to look for them. Frank Crossley was the sort of man who'd be quite capable of engineering an accident — a common enough occurrence in this new, tough country.

'Where the devil do you two think you're off to? I wondered why you'd slunk off . . . '

'I — we're going to Northam. Tom and I need new boots.'

'Come into money have you? Or have you found some of mine? How're you getting to Northam? It's a fair old walk — and what's in that bag?'

'I thought we'd get a lift — on the road — and as for money, I was going to sell a few things I brought with me from home.' Alice was amazed how easily the inventions came to her lips, but Frank Crossley wasn't fooled for a second.

'Lies! A whole pack. I'll thank you, miss, to get back and see to your work indoors, and my children — and you, young fella, back out to that fencing, and don't think of trying anything on.'

Tom stood his ground mutinously, and Frank unslung his rifle.

'Tom! Do as he says,' Alice called out as her brother made a move towards Frank's horse. 'Leave him — don't — ' She screamed as Frank fired in the air.

Tom leaped back, and the horse reared and wheeled.

'That was just a warning. Next time — I'll get you. Now, do as I say.'

'I won't.' Tom darted behind the horse. 'You can't order us about — and you can't put us in prison like Jim!'

'What are you saying?' Frank reined his horse in tightly.

'It's nothing. He's making it up.' Alice ran between them as Frank turned his horse and raised his rifle. 'Run. Run, Tom. Run away. Find Ned.'

She heard a drumming of hooves, and in a flashing mêlée of horses and riders, saw the gun fly from Frank's hand. Ned leaped off his horse and pulled Frank down to the ground. They rolled over and over, Ned's face dark with anger, Frank mouthing oaths.

Alice watched in horror as Ned's fist drew back and swung into Frank's jaw. There was a sickening crack as his body went slack, his head dropping to one side.

Ned leaned over, put his hand against Frank's neck, and nodded. 'He won't stop you leaving now. Alice, up behind me. Tom, run as fast as you can. The carriage is down the track. I heard the shot and unhitched the horse. Now hurry. The train's due from Northam in an hour.'

Alice stood unmoving. 'Frank? The children? I can't . . . '

'Yes, Alice, you can. Frank's only stunned. He'll come round in a few minutes. I'll send a message home from Northam. Aunt Edie'll send someone to make sure the youngsters are all right. I've found out — Jim is in Fremantle Prison. You'll be able to see him tomorrow.'

* * *

Ned arranged everything. A first-class train ticket to Fremantle, a coach to take them to a small hotel near the prison and, to her great joy, his Aunt Nellie, from Albany, waiting for them there.

'Ned insisted I came to chaperone you, my dear and truth to tell, I didn't need much persuasion. It's a delight for me to travel a little, although Ned's told me of the circumstances, which aren't pleasant for you. In the morning I'm to accompany you to the prison. An interview's been arranged with your young man, Jim. Tom shall escort me around the town, then we'll have lunch with my brother, Herbert — he's the lawyer, and will see what's to be done. I believe he's seeing the governor this morning.'

Alice wondered how many more aunts and uncles Ned McCartney had, but her heart brimmed with gratitude to them all. It was wonderful to be free of Frank Crossley, though she did worry about Elsie and Joey.

But, next morning, everything at Crossley's was driven from her head as she waited in a tiny, windowless room in Fremantle Prison. Her hands were damp, her breathing rapid, and she was frightened of fainting, so terror-struck was she by the thought of Jim, incarcerated in this dreadful, gloomy place.

'Must know someone, your chap,' the warder had commented as he led her to the visitors' room. 'Very rare for prisoners to be allowed private visits, especially from solitary.'

'Solitary?' Horror gripped her soul.

'Peterson, ain't it? Never out of solitary, for one thing or another. Shouldn't wonder if he ain't blind by now! You wait here, miss. Shan't be long.'

To Alice it seemed like hours since the warder's grisly comments. It was hot in the airless room, but at least she'd be free to leave, to walk in the sweet air outside, once she'd seen . . .

The door opened, the warder ushered in a stranger, who blinked unseeingly at her — a thin, gaunt man, with close-cropped hair, dressed in arrow-striped, shapeless grey. He shuffled forward, prodded from behind.

'Come on, Peterson. Greet the lady. She's come a fair distance to see you. London, ain't it, miss?'

She nodded, choking back the tears. She hadn't cried once since leaving home, but how could the tears be staunched at this pitiful sight? Jim Peterson, the dark-haired, laughing boy had vanished. What awful thing had brought him to this? She swallowed back the tears. They were no use to Jim, and it was her strength he needed.

'Jim!' She put out both her hands and took his.

'No touching of the prisoner, miss. Now, either side of the table. I'll stay by the door. Just pretend I'm not here.'

'Can't we be alone?'

'Against the rules. Just ignore me.' He nudged his prisoner. 'Sit down.'

Jim stared at him, then at Alice. He rubbed the back of his hand across his eyes, and looked again. 'Alice? Is it Alice? Alice Foster, from home?' Even his voice was different; thin and reedy. He sat down heavily, eyes fixed on her.

'Yes, it's truly me — Alice. You wrote, asking me to come to Australia, Jim, to marry you. You remember?'

'Yes — but that was before . . . nearly a year ago. My God . . . Alice . . . you came all that way and now . . . '

She saw the utter despair in his eyes, before he dropped his head, hiding his desolation from her.

'Tell me, Jim. What happened — why are you here?'

He was silent for a long time. The warder looked at his watch.

'Jim,' she prompted, 'tell me what happened. I — we — can help you.'

It seemed an age before he raised his head. 'How long have you been here?'

'I came with Tom — about two months ago. Never mind that now. Tell me what happened to you. Was it Frank Crossley?'

'You know him?'

'We — Tom and I — had to stay there.'

'You went there? To the Crossley place?'

Alice could see his agony deepening. 'Jim,' she spoke sharply, 'you must tell me quickly. I . . . I may not be able to come again for a while. I'm here, I'm all right, and I'm not going back to Crossley's — but if we're to help you, you've got to talk to me.'

'But, Alice, I swear I didn't know you

were coming. All this — ' He gestured despairingly round the room. 'This happened just after I'd written asking you to join me. I wrote from prison, too, but — the mail's, well, uncertain.' He glanced at the prison officer.

'Go on.'

'It was true, what I wrote to you. I had a good gold strike. Enough to set us up — but I was greedy. I wanted more. I can't tell you . . . '

'You have to.' Alice was stern, although her being ached with pity for him.

He took courage from her resolution, squared his shoulders, and met her gaze directly. 'I'll tell you the truth. I'm a gambler, Alice. I had to leave England in a hurry because of gambling debts. I could never tell you, or your family. I thought . . . a clean break . . . start again! And, for a while, I didn't gamble — no cards, no betting. I worked hard. Got a job here in Fremantle, saved a bit so I could go to the goldfields. Then the worst thing in my life happened.'

Hatred and bitterness contorted his face. 'I met Frank Crossley in a bar here. He was looking for labour, promised me a good wage, better than I was getting. I fell for it, left my job here and went to Northam, to the Crossley farm. You've seen the place — and Frank — so you know what it — he's like, but he promised me a bonus when his wheat cropped. So I worked, and waited. It wasn't too bad. Eve was a good cook. A good woman — why she married Crossley I'll never know.

'While she was alive, he just about kept on the right side of the law. But he ran a gambling game, after Eve's death. She wasn't cut out for the hard life, just gave up. Anyway, Frank's game was very dubious. There were often ugly fights, so I cleared off, without pay, to Kalgoorlie. That's where I struck it rich, and wrote to you.' A faint glimmer of a smile fleetingly recalled the young man she'd so passionately adored as a young girl. 'I always remembered you — so pretty and so so neat. And a hard worker. I thought we could make a go of it here.' The smile vanished. Dark memories clouded his eyes.

'And?' Alice had to prompt.

'And then I made an even bigger mistake. I actually went back to Frank's, with my gold. Thought I could beat him at his own game.' He banged his fists on the table. 'Alice, how could I have been such a fool? But Eve had died. It was chaos there . . . those poor kids . . . and the games and gambling were wild. Rogues and sharpers from miles around. Frank and his cronies took me for a ride. I had one drink — but, I swear to this day — Frank had put something in it. I remember starting to play, then someone accused me of cheating. All hell broke loose. I must have been hit on the head, and the next thing I knew I was in Northam jail accused of attempted murder. One of Frank's friends had been stabbed — nearly died — if he had, I'd have been hanged, no doubt, by now.' He reached for Alice's hands.

The warder stared impassively above their heads.

'I swear to you, Alice, I didn't do it. I didn't even have a knife.'

'But if you were innocent . . . '

'Alice, Alice.' Jim shook his head. 'Don't you know the world, the Frank Crossleys? Of course, my money had disappeared, my claim lost. Frank's friends swore on oath I'd lost any money I'd had legitimately at cards, and that I'd turned violent and stabbed this fellow in revenge. They all stuck together against me.'

'Couldn't you appeal?'

'There's more. Frank has a cousin here.' He lowered his voice to a whisper that only Alice could hear. 'A prison officer. After the trial, I was so furious at the injustice of it all, I went wild, and this officer made sure I was up in solitary, and again, when I'd done my time — and again — any trumped-up charge. I got a reputation. I'm powerless, Alice. I can't see anyone, can't do anything. Crossley and his cronies, they've got me in here for life. I couldn't believe it when the governor sent word I had a visitor. I never dreamed it'd be you. Oh, Alice, what have I brought you to? How're you managing?'

She put her fingers to his lips. 'Ssh. I'll tell you all about that sometime. But you're not to worry any more. You've got friends outside now. Powerful ones — the McCartneys.'

She told him all about meeting Ned on the boat, and how good he'd been to Tom. 'And Ned's brother's a lawyer here. He's to see you later, and Ned'll come, too. So, you must have courage, and I hope, Jim, if what you've told me is the truth, you've nothing to fear.'

'It is, I swear. I'm weak and foolish, but I'm no liar. You must believe me.'

Alice looked at him, and read in his eyes all the things he'd said. He was weak and foolish, she saw that now. After Ned — but she mustn't think of him. Jim needed her help so much.

'You do believe me,' he repeated,

'and when — if — I ever get out of this rotten, corrupt hole, you'll help me, won't you? You'll not leave me? You won't go back to London . . . I couldn't bear it. You've no idea what it's like in here. You must help me!' His eyes pleaded, his body tensed.

The prison officer came to life.

'That's all the time you'll get on this visit, Peterson.'

'Alice?'

'Yes, I'll help you, Jim. Now, and after you come out.'

10

In the hotel that evening, Tom and Nellie McCartney did their best to raise Alice's spirits, but her visit to Fremantle Prison, Jim's plight, and her own uncertain future, and Tom's, weighed too heavily upon her.

Tom was full of his day's outing with Nellie. The bustling town and port, so strange when they'd first docked on SS Pathan, was now, he boasted, home from home. It'd be a fine town to find work and settle in, he told his sister, youthfully optimistic about their future.

'And we called in at the P & O offices. Aunt Nellie's idea, and guess what, Alice? This'll cheer you up.' He produced a thick envelope. 'I was saving it for a surprise. A letter from home — it's addressed to both of us, but I thought you should open it.'

'That was kind of you, Tom, but you can open it. We'll read it together, if Aunt Nellie doesn't mind?'

'Bless you, no. Tom's told me so much about your family today, I feel they're old friends already. Quickly, Tom, I long to know how your father is.'

'Are all the McCartney's as kind as you?' Alice smiled, comforted by Nellie's warm motherliness.

'There are a lot of us, so I expect we have a few rogues or skeletons in the cupboards, but Ned keeps us in order. Ever since his father died, he's taken on the head-of-the-household rôle. That's one of the reasons he came back from Europe. We missed him so much — but do read your letter. You'll not be wanting to hear all about the McCartneys.'

But I do, Alice's heart said, unbidden, making her blush at the shameful thought that she could listen to anything about Ned for hour upon hour! Tom slit the envelope and pulled out sheets of notepaper, handing them to Alice.

'Here, you're a faster reader. Tell us the news.'

She scanned the pages rapidly, sometimes with a smile, then a frown.

'Bertha's doing well at Rivingtons. The boys are well — Dad's still got his job. Oh, dear, his chest is bad, and Bertha fears for the coming winter.' She laid the letter on her lap. 'They want to know when they can fix a time to come out here.' The tears, never far away today, after seeing Jim, were hard to hold back.

'Let them come,' Tom said stoutly. 'We'll manage somehow.'

'Tom, it's not so easy, not now.' She turned to Nellie. 'We owe you and Ned so much. I don't know what we'll do — and how can we tell Father that Jim's in prison? No farm, no job, no money — '

'Now, Alice, don't give way. You've been so strong — all that trouble at the Crossley place. I told Ned in Albany, he

193

never should have let you go there. But that's all done with now. We must look to the future; see what's to be done about your poor, young man in that dreadful place. Herbert's no doubt got the facts. He'll be in touch with Ned, and Ned'll be here soon.'

'But how can I pay for all this? Lawyers — all I owe to Ned?'

'Oh, Alice. We've got lots of money. I'm a rich, old spinster — let me have a bit of fun. I've so enjoyed my day with Tom. Don't spoil it all by worrying about money. Jim's case may take some while. We'll move to lodgings if you like, and if it makes you happy, you can be my housekeeper.' She testily waved away Alice's thanks. 'If you want to do something useful, you'll sit down and write to your family and tell them what the situation is, but don't be gloomy, child. Something'll turn up. It always does.'

So Alice wrote an honest letter to her family in London. She tried to make it as hopeful as she could, but sensed it lacked conviction.

With a sigh, she put down the pen. 'Here, Tom, you write a line. Tell them all the nice things you can about Australia.'

'That's easy, but it'd take too long.'

Alice laughed for the first time that day. Thank goodness for young Tom!

She was much cheered next day to learn that Herbert McCartney had seen the prison governor, got Jim out of solitary confinement, had a long talk with him, and was looking into his case. The best news was that Ned's mother was better and Ned himself would be coming to Fremantle in two days' time.

Two days never dragged so slowly. Alice asked if she could visit Jim, but Herbert McCartney had sent word that it wouldn't be advisable just yet.

Ned appeared when they were at supper, and as soon as his broad frame appeared in the dining-room doorway, Alice felt that all may yet be well. He was smiling, his blue eyes seeking hers, reassuring, calming. He'd seen his

Uncle Herbert — they were to meet again the next day at the prison, and would all see Jim together. They went upstairs to the small, private sitting-room, and Ned told them the good news about his mother. She was well enough for him to be away. Tilly and his brother were taking good care of her.

'Now, Alice, about Jim Peterson. You've seen him?'

She nodded. 'It was dreadful. I hardly knew him. He told me — '

'I know. Herbert has the whole story. And Crossley's disappeared. The farm's deserted.'

'Elsie? Joey?'

He took her hand. 'Don't worry, they're with his sister in York. She's a good woman, with children of her own. She wanted to take them when Eve Crossley died, but Frank wouldn't let them go.'

'But where is he? And how can we prove Jim's innocence?'

'Already done. It wasn't difficult. I tracked down some of Crossley's associates. As soon as they heard he'd disappeared, one or two were eager to talk — for a consideration, of course! Seems the idea was to rob Jim — the fight was an accident, but Frank saw it as a good way of disposing of Jim. Someone else did the stabbing, but they all stuck together to blame Jim — so they could divide up the money. We may even be lucky and get some of it back.'

'That would be wonderful. I — we — could repay you.'

Ned frowned. 'That's not necessary. I've told you before.'

There was a moment of tension between them. Nellie looked from one to the other, a worried frown on her kind face.

'And — er — why ever did Mr Crossley send for Alice in the first place?

'That we won't know unless he tells us — when he's caught, which he will be eventually, and stands trial for perverting the course of justice. I guess he saw Alice as a cheap housekeeper. He does at least show some concern for his children. A young girl, all alone, out from England — he could do what he liked.'

'Ned, don't!' Nellie shuddered.

'I should never have stayed so long,' Alice said hastily, 'but the children . . .'

'You didn't have a lot of choice. Frank's mates told me they had instructions to stay away completely — until he'd got you thoroughly cowed I expect.'

'Poor, poor Jim. All those months — '

'It could have been years. Jim never had a chance to put his case, and Frank's cousin intercepted any letters Jim tried to send out.'

'How long till we can get him free?' Alice thought of the future.

'I don't know. As soon as we have sworn statements from the men at the gambling game, Jim could be out, and he'll certainly be given a less harsh régime at the prison in the meantime. I'm going to see Herbert now. I'll collect you in the morning, Alice, to go to the prison. We should know more by then.'

Alice slept little that night. The oppressive weight of Jim's situation had lifted, and Elsie and Joey were safe. She had much to give thanks for. But her own plight! That was the problem, for Alice knew, had known subconsciously almost from the first day she'd set eyes on him on the London dock, that Ned McCartney was the man she loved — deeply and truly. Yet, she was promised to Jim Peterson, and after all he'd gone through, how could she refuse? She had to remain true to Jim. She dared not even consider how Ned felt about her. That must never even be dreamed about.

Yet when Ned handed her into the carriage for the short drive to the prison next morning, she found it impossible not to be aware of his burning glances, and when he took her hand, she knew what he was going to say.

'The prison looks less forbidding

today — the sunshine — ' She floundered.

'Alice, look at me.' He turned her to him. 'You know what I will say. You're no fool, and too honest not to admit what there is between us. I know you are promised to Jim, but you should not marry unless you love him. I thought long and hard last night. The honourable thing would be for me to go away, never to tell you what is in my heart. I find it impossible to do that. I love you too much, Alice. I cannot imagine a future without you. Before you are committed to Jim, dishonourable or not . . . '

His mouth claimed hers, this time as a confessed lover, masterful and persuasive. Alice received his kiss, and returned it with bitter-sweet despair. She loved him! He loved her! But Jim's fate lay between them. How could she abandon her duty and promise? Ned had so much, a loving family, position, wealth — Jim had nothing.

The carriage drew up outside the

stone-arched outer gate. Ned and Alice clung together, then parted slowly.

Ned said, 'Don't say it, Alice. I know your decision. It's in your face.'

She cried out, 'What can I do? When you see him . . . it would be so cruel. Crueller even than all Frank Crossley's actions. I cannot — we could never be happy, knowing . . . '

'I think we could, but I respect your decision. I won't make it harder for you. If all goes well this morning, I shall return to Koolingup Farm. If I stayed near you, I would not be able to stand by and let you marry Peterson.'

His face was harsh, closed, and, Alice felt, crushed and broken. This was far, far worse than anything she had ever suffered before.

Throughout the interview with Herbert McCartney, a bluff, kindly male equivalent of Aunt Nell, Alice heard not a word. Jim had improved beyond recognition, and it was easy to recall the old Jim Peterson of so many years ago. Hope had put the life back in him, and he glanced across at Alice with gratitude. Ned sat silent while Herbert went over all the ground again.

Finally, he asked his nephew, 'Ned, anything I haven't covered? Anything to say to Jim?'

Ned looked up, frowning darkly. With an effort he said, 'No, I'm pleased your innocence is proved. I think you'll be freed very soon. If I, or my family, can help, we will, with jobs or anything at all.' He stood up abruptly. 'I'll leave now, Uncle Herbert. If there's anything . . . ' He was already by the door.

Alice half rose, his name on her lips unuttered. She sank back, trying to still her trembling hands, remembering the feel of Ned's lips on hers.

'Just a second, Ned, I'd like to ask . . . ' Herbert followed him out of the room, and Alice was left alone with Jim.

He looked strangely at her. 'Alice? What is it? Aren't you happy? We can be together soon . . . build our lives . . . begin afresh.'

'Yes,' she whispered. 'I'm — I'm very happy.'

The warder sidled into the room. 'Can't leave you two alone. Didn't realise your lawyer wasn't here.'

Jim ignored him. 'Alice — there's something wrong. Tell me.'

'I — I can't. Don't ask me.'

'Quickly now — the truth. You asked for that from me before, now it's your turn. You and that fellow, Ned. There's something between you — you're in love. You are, aren't you? With him — not me at all? Truth, Alice.'

'Yes, then, but I'll stay with you . . . I promised.'

Jim buried his head in his hands.

Alarmed, she stood up.

Jim was rocking back and forth, but to Alice's amazement, when he raised his head, she saw he was laughing!

'I'm — I'm sorry,' Jim said, 'but it's funny — after all this time. Alice, there's no time to lose — quick, run after that fellow. I release you from your promise. When I heard the news from the lawyer about Crossley being found out, my innocence proved at last . . . well . . . everything changed. I would have married you, but, I'm ashamed to say, I wrote to you on a whim, meaning it at the time, and never thinking it would have led you to end up at that place. I like you, admire you more than any girl in the whole world, but I don't want to marry. I want to go back to the goldfields — be free again. This time I'll make my fortune. I've learned my lesson, you'll see. With a wife, however wonderful, I couldn't do it. I'd be tied. Don't lose him. Oh, Alice! Both you and I thinking the same — of sacrificing — for the sake of the other! Thank God your feelings are written so plain on your face. McCartney's a very lucky fellow. Go on, Alice — to your Ned!'

She rushed over, kissed him soundly on the cheek, and flew out of the room, bumping into Uncle Herbert coming in.

'Where's Ned?' she demanded.

'Just gone — I — '

Alice ran along the corridors, wings on her feet.

'Ned, Ned, wait — don't go!' She reached the outer gate. 'Ned!'

Alice flung herself at the departing coach. The driver turned, startled. Ned opened the door, leaped out, and seized Alice in his arms.

'I love you — Jim doesn't — so it's all right. I can marry you — please — if you want. Jim doesn't want to — '

Ned swept her off her feet, pressing her tightly to him. 'I couldn't have let you go. I'd have carried you off by force if necessary, but this way is better.' He swung her up into his arms. 'You'd better get into the coach with me, before we shock the good citizens of Fremantle right here on the streets.'

Once inside the carriage he kissed her, then put a small, velvet pouch into her hand.

'I wanted to return this to you with my love and my heart. Your mother's wedding ring. Wear it for me until I place my ring on your finger at our wedding.' He took the gold band from her and put it on her finger, his dark-blue eyes searching hers. 'I love you, Alice, and soon we'll bring all your family out to Australia, to share our happiness.'

Alice, too full of emotion to speak, simply lifted her face to his, and as the carriage rattled away from the grey walls of Fremantle prison into the sunshine, the lovers kissed, pledging their everlasting love for each other.

Alice's dangerous journey was ended; a happier one was about to begin.

THE END

We do hope that you have enjoyed reading this large print book.

Did you know that all of our titles are available for purchase?

We publish a wide range of high quality large print books including:
Romances, Mysteries, Classics
General Fiction
Non Fiction and Westerns

Special interest titles available in large print are:
The Little Oxford Dictionary
Music Book, Song Book
Hymn Book, Service Book

Also available from us courtesy of Oxford University Press:
Young Readers' Dictionary
(large print edition)
Young Readers' Thesaurus
(large print edition)

For further information or a free brochure, please contact us at:
Ulverscroft Large Print Books Ltd.,
The Green, Bradgate Road, Anstey,
Leicester, LE7 7FU, England.
Tel: (00 44) **0116 236 4325**
Fax: (00 44) **0116 234 0205**

THREE TALL TAMARISKS

Christine Briscomb

Joanna Baxter flies from Sydney to run her parents' small farm in the Adelaide Hills while they recover from a road accident. But after crossing swords with Riley Kemp, life is anything but uneventful. Gradually she discovers that Riley's passionate nature and quirky sense of humour are capturing her emotions, but a magical day spent with him on the coast comes to an abrupt end when the elegant Greta intervenes. Did Riley love Greta after all?

SUMMER IN HANOVER SQUARE

Charlotte Grey

The impoverished Margaret Lam-
bart is suddenly flung into all the
glitter of the Season in Regency
London. Suspected by her god-
mother's nephew, the influential
Marquis St. George, of being merely
a common adventuress, she has,
nevertheless, a brilliant success, and
attracts the attentions of the young
Duke of Oxford. However, when the
Marquis discovers that Margaret is
far from wanting a husband he finds
he has to revise his estimate of her
true worth.

CONFLICT OF HEARTS

Gillian Kaye

Somerset, at the end of World War I: Daniel Holley, unhappily married to an ailing wife and father of four grown-up children, is attracted to beautiful schoolteacher Harriet Bray, but he knows his love is hopeless. Daniel's only daughter, Amy, who dreams of becoming a milliner and is caught up in her love for young bank clerk John Tottle, looks on as the drama of Daniel and Harriet's fate and happiness gradually unfolds.